To Bring Him Home

A Generation Son Chronicle

Book 3

By

C.J. Rose

This book is dedicated to those who fight every day for love, life, laughter, and what they believe in.

The Road So Far...

I wake up every day with a piece missing from my heart. Not a moment goes by that the death of my mother doesn't rip at me. I have nightmares repeatedly, of the look on her face when he plunged the sword into her chest. It's not an image one can easily forget.

Bethany decided to stay in our mother's room instead of her own, leaving Gwen to reside in her old room. It didn't take much to do a little rearranging of personal belongings. The Guardians have kept to their word and we have not had to worry about financial matters.

The guardian working with Bethany while we were in France is now living in Gwen's apartment. She checks in on us daily and works with Bethany a few times a week. She is not much older than we are, but you can tell she has put in her time already. Bethany's skills are improving, but she is far from ready, though I have to admit, she is catching on a lot quicker than I did. Gwen and I continue our own form of training as much as time allows. Schoolwork, housework, and adult responsibilities take up a good amount of our time.

We made it through, but Christmas is another day for us now. Neither of us had a desire to celebrate anything even though the guardians made a feast in Gwen's old apartment and gifts were exchanged. The mood was somber and as soon as we were done eating and unwrapping, we went our separate ways.

School; not long after everything was squared away, we had to sit down with the school counselor and a guardian. We were excused for school for what we had missed, and considering the circumstances, they let everything else slide. As my mother said, the students have been broken up into junior high schools. The seniors, however, are able to stay in the main building to finish their classes while they work on repairs to the high school.

Lucky for Gwen and I there is not a lot of time left for us there. With everything else, we were given the opportunity to graduate early as long as our credits are in. Gwen is early anyway, so she is in good shape, but I will need to take a few extra classes to make it happen. Therefore, if all goes well, we will be out no later than January 22. Trust me when I say, I will make this happen.

My guidance counselor recommended a correspondence course that will give me a half credit. With my regular schedule and two correspondence courses, I will get back on track. The plan is to make sure nothing, or no one gets in the way. It includes any gods, musketeers, or anyone else who thinks they can come into my life right now.

Well ok then...

It's almost the end of the semester, and I can see Bethany is pushing herself to make it through. Sometimes I want her to stop training, but I know if I try, she will only resent my need to be a fill-in parent.

I can't think of her as my baby sister, knowing she has gone through so much trauma, which no teenager should experience in such a short period. As I watch her, I can't help but feel a deep sense of regret for not being what she needs right now.

"Do you have homework?"

"No."

"Are you training tonight?"

"No."

"Are you going to finish your food?"

"No."

I am seeing a pattern. "Do you want to dance with the devil in the pale moonlight?"

"Batman? Really?"

"It got your attention didn't it?"

"I am fine. You don't need to ask me a million questions a million times a day." She pushes her chair fiercely into the table and storms off to her room.

"Well, that was subtle." Gwen has stayed quiet this whole time.

"Well, what else am I supposed to do?"

"Give her time. Can you honestly tell me you are truly okay right now?" She stares me down, waiting for my answer, but already knowing what it is.

"No."

"Can you give me a reason why she should be over it?"

"No."

"Are you going to give me an actual answer, Bethany?"

"Not funny!"

"Easy there, killer. You may be the joker who can't take a joke, but I've proven my point."

She remains quiet while I pick at my food.

"I know."

"Leave her be. You know she has always been her own person. She will grieve on her own terms. She will heal in her own time. She will grow. On. Her. Own." She put emphasis on the last few words.

Bethany sits in her room curled up under her mother's blanket. She holds the locket in her hand, and randomly opens it, looking at the pictures of her mother and father on the inside. She strokes her mother's face, feeling something rigid underneath. Bethany battles in her mind on whether or not to pull the picture out and see what is behind it.

She reaches for a small metal nail file to lift the picture out. Bethany kisses the oval paper and places it to the side. It's at that moment she knows she will never be without her mother again.

"Luthor!" Her voice carries through the apartment.

My first instinct is to grab my sword, but it's not there. Gwen and I jump from our chairs, running to Bethany's room, but she flings open the door before we can reach it and meets halfway.

"Look!" It's the first time, in a long time, I have seen a genuine smile on her face.

"What?"

"Look!" She shows me the locket.

"It's a locket."

"Really? Let me see." Gwen shoves me out of the way. She pauses a moment before her words change their tone, "Oh my."

"What?"

"The locket, it's like." She trails off.

"It's like what?" I flap my arms for her to continue.

"See for yourself" Bethany hands it to me.

I look it over and see she has taken the picture of our mother out. Before I can ask her why, I answer my own question. There is a tiny button the size of a grain of dried rice right in the center. I go to place my finger on it when I hear Bethany call out in a panic. "No!"

"What?"

"Don't you dare. Don't you dare take this moment away from me." I can see tears welling up in her eyes.

"I am sorry." I bend my head and hand her the locket.

"Shall we?" She looks up at the two of us.

Gwen and I throw a quick glance at each other. Then, we turn to Bethany, and both say, in unison, "Yes!"

Making her way back into the room, Bethany takes the locket and places it on the edge of the bed. We brace ourselves as she reaches to press the button. As soon as she does, a burst of golden light fills the room. We guard our eyes until its light fades enough to focus.

There she is, a figure in white, looking exactly like she did when she died. Her long red hair flows behind her, and the burial gown they chose for her flutters in the imaginary breeze.

"Mom."

My mother reaches a ghostly hand towards Bethany's cheek to wipe away her tears, but it simply goes through her face. "I am so sorry." My mother cries.

"Sorry? Why are you sorry?"

"For this."

"You have no reason to be sorry, Catherine." Gwen speaks up.

"My sweet, Gwen."

"Mother." Bethany brings my mother's attention back to her, "I miss you."

"I miss you too. I am so happy you figured it out. Like Luthor's watch, you now have your own way to be in touch with me."

"Will the watch work to speak with you?"

"No, Luthor. Only one spirit can inhabit an object. The good thing is, if they are both activated, we can all speak to each other."

"You mean?" Bethany stops.

"Yes. If the watch and the locket are open at the same time, you will be able to speak with your father and me together, and your father and I can speak to each other. The only thing is, the buttons have to be pressed at the same time, or the balance between us will not be stable enough to communicate with each other."

"Mom?"

"Yes, Luthor?"

"Thank you."

"For what?"

"For everything." The three of us speak at once.

I can see the joy and pride in my mother's eyes as she looks at the three of us. "You three are my entire world. I hope what I did is enough." There is a pause before she speaks again. "I have to go. You three take care of each other."

"Mom!"

The light begins to fade as my mother turns to face Bethany. "I must go."

"I love you!" Bethany wipes her own tears away.

"I love you too." Her words fade out as the bright light dims, and the ghostly image of my mother is gone.

I stand there for a minute, taking it all in. It's the same feeling as discovering my father in the watch all over again. Gwen holds my hand and pulls me towards Bethany. We wrap each other in a warm, tight embrace.

"I hate hugs."

"No you don't." I squeeze Bethany tighter.

What's with the attitude?

The next day, Bethany knows she has to return to 'normal life'. She wakes up, gets herself ready, and prepares to head out the door for school. She clutches onto her locket with a newfound lease on life. During her first class, she catches herself fiddling with it, struggling with the temptation to press the tiny little button.

"Miss McAlester."

Bethany brings her focus back to class. The students turn in their desks to look at her. Instead of scrunching down in her seat, she raises her eyes to him and speaks with a confident tone, "Yes, Mr. Lancaster?"

"Now that I have your attention, please tell me the meaning of pneumonoultramicroscopicsilicovolcanoconiosis."

"Mr. Lancaster?" She looks at him inquisitively.

"If you have been paying attention, Miss McAlester, you will know this."

"If you weren't so boring, maybe I would."

The positive nature vanishes as if it were never there.

"Excuse me?"

"I said."

"I know what you said. I am wondering what makes you think you can."

"I am going to go with my juvenile delinquent tendencies, and my inability to listen to authority." She sits back and crosses her arms, waiting for a reply.

"The death of your mother doesn't excuse you from participation, nor does it give you leeway to mouth off to a teacher."

"Then maybe I shouldn't be here." She rises from her seat.

"Maybe you are correct. To the principal, now!"

"I think maybe I will go home instead."

She makes her way to the door. As one hand touches the handle, the other touches the locket. She turns to get in one final word. "The answer is lung disease."

"Excuse me?"

"The meaning of pneumonoultramicroscopicsilicovolcanoconiosis is lung disease." She walks out the door, closing it with a slam.

There is silence behind her for a moment until Mr. Lancaster begins to speak. "Well then, now that's done. I want you all to turn to page three hundred and ninety-four."

Bethany leans against the lockers and slowly slumps to the floor. Pulling her knees in, she cries until the bell rings.

She opens the door slowly to the office, steps inside, and pans the room for the receptionist. "Miss McAlester." her sweet voice comes from behind the desk, "What can I." She breaks off. "Sweetie, have you been crying? Come here and sit down."

The secretary comes around the desk and pats the couch.

"I am fine Mrs. Goosebottom." Bethany wipes away one more tear.

"Well then, what can I do for you?"

Bethany looks in her eyes and can almost see a different person. "The principal."

"I am sorry dear, I don't understand."

"I was sent to see the principal by Mr. Lancaster."

"Oh, that mean old brute; one minute."

She walks away, leaving Bethany sitting there. Taking a few deep breaths to calm herself, the door to the principal's office creaks open and he comes out to meet her. He is new to the school, taller than the last principal, much better looking, and younger. His hair sits flat on top of his head and scruff covering his face makes him look a little more rugged. If you take away the suit and the beard, he can't be more than twenty-three.

"Miss McAlester, I presume. Come in then."

He has a slight British accent as he speaks, and she follows him into the office and sits in one of the leather-bound chairs opposite his desk.

"What can I do for you?" He reaches for a pen and begins to write something, but she can't tell what.

"Mr. Lancaster, sir."

"What about him?"

"I told him off, sir."

"Oh, enough with the sir. Call me Mr. Testerman."

He gets up and makes his way to the other side of the desk. He sits on the edge facing Bethany and his position makes her feel uncomfortable. She shifts in the chair slightly before speaking.

"Yes, sir." She pulls the locket out of her shirt and begins moving it between her fingers.

"Mr. Testerman."

"Yes, Mr. Testerman."

"Better, now tell me what happened."

It takes a few moments to begin the story, but once she is finished, she ends the story with the description of how she felt after shutting the door to Mr. Lancaster's classroom. "I am not going to lie, this may not be the last time I am in this office."

"I see, and why is that?"

"Because, I hate it here." She crosses her arms.

"Don't we all?" He chuckles as he makes his way back behind the desk. Sitting down, he takes a pen and begins to write again. "Here is what I will do, since I am a man of chances, I am going to let this one slide. If I see you in here again at all this week, I will have no choice but to give you a detention. You know the rules; three detentions equal a three-day suspension. Are you willing to risk your last two years of school?"

"I've already risked more."

"So be it, but you have been warned. Take this and get back to class."

Bethany leaves the office with a pass and makes her way to class. At least this time, she knows the teacher will be someone a little more sympathetic to her situation. Mrs. Granada lost her mother not too long ago too.

"Mrs. Granada." She enters the room and hands her the pass.

"Thank you, Bethany. Please, take your seat."

"Class, I want you to take a moment to consider something."

She stops and makes her way to the board. Picking up a piece of chalk, she begins to write a word in bold letters; PAIN. A student raises his hand, and without even waiting for her to respond, begins to speak, "Mrs. Granada, what does pain have to do with the crusades?"

"More than you think, Melvin." She continues to write, as the chalk dust covers the board.

Melvin; Mr. Know-It-All, being put in his place as usual. No matter how many times it happens, he continues to question everything. Bethany shrugs it off with a snicker as a nauseous feeling comes over her. Placing her hands over her mouth, she stands and runs to the wastebasket at the back of the room.

"Bethany?"

"I am okay."

"Why don't you go to the restroom? Guiney, why don't you go with her?"

Guiney rises from her desk and makes her way to Bethany's side. "Come on."

They make it to the bathroom with no loss of bodily fluids. Bethany turns on the cold water and begins to splash her face. Looking up in the mirror she can see the black lines running down the middle of my cheeks.

"Here." Guiney hands her a face wipe.

"You seriously keep makeup wipes in your purse?"

"Who doesn't?"

"You are something else. I don't suppose you have a medicine cabinet hiding in there too, do you?"

"Why as a matter of fact." Guiney trails off, reaching into her purse. She pulls out a small pouch and begins to pull out a variety of bottles.

"Good lord, do you have a whole pharmacy in there?"

"No, just a few necessities." She is still pulling bottles out.

"The magic bag from Harry Potter? Do you have Hermione Granger in there?"

Bethany laughs so hard she begins to feel lightheaded again. As she begins to drop, Guiney catches her before hitting the floor.

"Woah." Guiney catches her head.

"Thanks."

"What are friends for?" Guiney slowly lifts her to a sitting position, "What is going on with you?"

"I have no idea, but help me up."

Once Guiney gets Bethany back to her feet, they both make their way to the nurse's office. Guiney leaves and heads back to class.

"Well, Miss McAlester, I haven't seen you here in a long time. What's going on?"

"Just feeling lightheaded and nauseous."

"What have you eaten today? Drink?"

"Nothing."

"No wonder you aren't feeling well. Give me a minute and I will be right back."

The nurse leaves the room and goes into her office. It's not long before she comes back out with a cup of something and a granola bar. She hands it to Bethany and insists she consume it all.

Taking one sip, she immediately spits it out. "What is this?"

"A little concoction of my own design."

"It tastes like cow piss."

"I don't want to know how you figured out what cow piss tastes like." The nurse rolls her eyes.

"Sorry." She takes a sip again, doing her best to swallow, "Seriously, what is in this?"

"A few herbs, a little water, brewed almost like tea."

"I will forever dislike tea now."

"Now, now, I know it may not taste the best, but trust me. You will feel much better once you finish it. Make sure you eat, too."

She points to the granola bar before walking away leaving Bethany sitting alone. Sip by nasty sip, she finishes the drink, taking small bites of the granola bar to help erase the taste.

Finished, she hops down from the table and makes her way to the to find the nurse. A smell hits her nose before she even touches the door, but doesn't see the nurse anywhere. "Ms. Easegrom?"

"Yes, dear?" She comes up from behind, startling Bethany.

"I thought you were in your office."

"Oh no, dear, I am right here. What is it?"

Easegrom's shoulders are set back, a little tense, and her eyes are dilated. You can see the red veins weaving their way through the white area surrounding her pupils. A smell resonated from her person, not like the tea, but stronger, almost metallic; like blood.

"Nothing, I wanted to tell you I am feeling better." She inches her way past Ms. Easegrom, easing towards the door.

"Are you sure you are alright, you look a little peckish?"

"I am fine. I need to eat a little more. It's almost lunch time." Her voice shakes slightly.

Before the nurse can say another word, Bethany's hand catches the doorknob and she makes her way out, keeping an eye on Ms. Easegrom the whole time. The expression changes gradually as her lips curl on one side, and her eyes become brighter and more intense.

Bethany shuts the door behind her and runs back to class.

Once she makes it back to class, she stops, catching her breath and composing herself before walking in to take her seat.

"Are you feeling better?"

"Yes, Mrs. Granada, thank you."

"Good. Guiney can catch you up later. Now, let's turn our attention to the board."

Mrs. Granada's words trail off as Bethany looks towards Guiney to grab her attention, motioning to her phone. Reaching in her backpack, Guiney lifts her phone and waits for the message.

Bethany begins to type, keeping the phone hidden under her desk, but her eyes focused on the board. Swipe after frantic swipe, she begins to write out what happened in the nurse's office. Hitting send, she places her phone in her pocket and waits for Guiney to read it.

Her phone buzzes and Guiney does her best to hide it. "Whose is it?"

"Mine. It's my mother. May I be excused?"

"Make it quick." Mrs. Granada hesitates before turning back to the board and finishing her lesson.

Guiney makes her way to the hall and begins to read the message from me.

"It was the weirdest thing. After you left, she came in and gave me some weird drink. She said it was like tea, and it tasted horrible. After I took the first sip, she went into her office. I knew the only way I was going to leave was if I finished it, so I did. When I got up to tell her I was leaving, she wasn't in her office. I know I saw her walk in, but I didn't see her walk out. Suddenly, she was behind me. Where did she come from? That's not the weirdest part. She smelled; not like a BO kind of smell, but like blood, dirt, and plants. Her eyes were much bigger than normal too, and the look on her face went from sweet and nice to

sadistic and cruel. I didn't stay long enough to see any more. WHAT IS GOING ON?"

Guiney finishes reading and responds with one thing, *"IDK"*. She makes her way back into class and sits down. Mrs. Granada asks her if everything is okay. Keeping her eyes on me, Guiney responds, "I hope so."

Now everyone is home, and we sit around the table to eat dinner as we always do. Bethany's guardian has been cooking for us almost every night, and she isn't too bad at it. Tonight's featured course consists of pasta, meatballs, garlic bread, and salad. She is never there when we get home, but you can tell she takes some food with her after she is done.

We sit in silence for a while before I finally cave. "So, how was everyone's day?" All I get in response is a grunt. "Seriously?"

Bethany looks up at me and smiles. "I hate you, you know that, right?"

"Bethany!" Gwen speaks in shock.

"Wow, tell me how you really feel." I sit back in my chair, dropping the fork on the plate, the sound rings like a bell.

"It's pretty simple really. Because you had to go off and play the hero, mom is dead."

"How is this my fault? Did I ask for this? No! Did I want this life? No! Did I want her to die? No! Could I have stopped her from coming to France? Also, no!"

Bethany can see the look of pure horror on Gwen's face. She knows it's because of the way her and Luthor are speaking to each other.

I decide before I go any further, it's best I walk away. I excuse myself and walk out the door, leaving an awed Gwen and an angered Bethany behind. I make my way outside.

Meanwhile, Gwen and Bethany are able to have their own conversation. It's heated, but necessary.

"What has gotten into you? You do realize you are not the only one dealing with this, right?"

"Worry about yourself. I am sure you and Luthor are doing pretty well together."

"What is that supposed to mean?" Gwen begins to grow angry, which is rare for her.

"You know what it means. My mother is dead and the two of you are playing house. It's sickening to watch the two of you parade around here as if nothing happened. You are not, nor will you ever be my mother. He will never be my father. Stop trying to act as if you are."

Bethany begins to rise, but Gwen grabs her arm.

"You don't get to be the only one who speaks their mind. Sit down!"

Her expression changes to a mixture of disgust and fear as Bethany sits back in my seat.

"Is this where you tell me everything will be fine and you and Luthor are hurting too?"

"Enough! I may not be your mother, but I sure as hell whoop you like I am. If you want to try me, I have no problems putting you back in your place."

As Gwen speaks, she slowly raises herself from the chair, placing her hands firmly on the table. Leaning over her, Bethany begins to slouch below Gwen.

"Are you finished?"

"Not even close." Gwen backs away slightly, "You need to understand, young lady, as of right now I am the only mother figure you have. If you want to ruin it with your childish attitude and disrespectful nature, go right ahead. When it comes time for you to need someone, I won't be there."

"I have never asked you to be."

"No, you didn't, but your mother did. I intend to honor her request, but so help me God, I will have no problems breaking it if I have to." Gwen begins to clear the table. Surprisingly, Bethany stands to help her.

"I don't know how to deal with this." She begins through tears.

Gwen turns to face her. "For starters, this," she pauses and uses her finger to wave up and down, "needs to stop. You can't expect to push people away and be able to heal. If you burn every bridge, who will be left to catch you if you fall?"

"Then tell me what to do, because I don't know." Bethany finally breaks, her body slowly drops to the floor; her hands are wet from the tears. "I don't know what to do. Tell me what to do."

Gwen kneels beside her and holds me, snot and all.

"We can talk about this more after a good night's sleep."

Let's try this again...

The breakdown Bethany had last night was what she finally needed to get over the hump and deal with things a little more easily. She finds Guiney waiting by her locker like she does every morning.

"Feeling better?"

"Much."

"Good, because I have a surprise for you." Guiney's eyes grow wide and she can't contain her excitement.

"What is it?"

"It will not be a surprise if I tell you."

"Seriously?" Bethany rolls her eyes.

"Come on." Guiney drags her by the arm, almost causing her to trip.

As they come around the corner to an abrupt stop, there he stands, the boy Bethany has had a crush on for years. He slowly makes his way towards her, and even his walk is dreamy. As he glides closer, he pulls a rose out from behind his back, causing Bethany to blush as he hands it to her.

"Ms. McAlester, will you do me the honor of this dance?" He holds out a hand and gives a slight bow as the music begins to play.

It's not loud, but she knows the song. It's her favorite from her favorite Disney movie. Without giving Bethany a moment to respond, he grabs her by the hand, places the rose in-between his teeth and dips her. She squeals, unable to control her laughter at the thought of it all.

He lifts her back up, wraps his arms around her waist, and begins to move. Bethany closes her eyes for a second, taking it all in. Gabriel's breath tickles the hairs on her neck, and she can't stop the tingle making its way down her spine.

"Why are you doing this?"

"Doing what?" He smiles.

"Dancing with me."

"Well, if you don't want to dance." He starts pulling away.

"No!" Bethany pulls him back in, "How did you know this was my favorite song?"

"Lucky guess?"

"Right."

"I will find my way, I can go the distance." He begins to sing in her ear.

"I know every mile will be worth my while." Bethany continues.

"I will go the distance; I'll be right where I belong." They finish together.

"Winter Ball?"

"Of course."

Gabriel takes a deep look into her eyes. She can tell he wants to lean in and kiss her, but he knows everyone is watching. He pulls out his phone and hands it to Bethany as she pulls out her own and does the same. After they exchange numbers, he leaves a simple kiss on her cheek.

The crowd is already starting to disperse by then as Guiney leans against the locker, waiting for her best friend. "Surprise!"

"You knew about this?"

"Yup."

"How long has he been planning this?"

"A while."

"Way to keep a secret. Come on, we are already late for class."

"I took care of it too."

"Well, you think of everything, don't you?"

As they walk down the hallway, they end up running across Mrs. Easegrom looking disheveled and weak. Her face is pale, but her cheeks are pink. Her normal scrubs look like she rolled through a mud pit. While her pockets are torn, and she is only wearing one shoe. They run to her and see if they can be of any help. She has a slight limp, and you can tell she is in pain.

"Mrs. Easegrom, what happened?" Bethany reaches under to support her arm.

"A person in the office, fire, hand."

That's all she gets out before collapsing completely.

"I am grabbing the teacher."

"Hurry!"

Bethany opens the classroom door in a panic. "Mrs. Reigina, quick, Mrs. Easegrom!"

Mrs. Reigina drops her chalk and rushes out the door. She makes her way towards Mrs. Easegrom, dropping to her knees and sliding the rest of the way. She immediately cradles the nurse's head, checking for a pulse. "Her pulse is faint. What happened, Bethany?"

"No idea. We were heading to class, and we ran into her like this. She was mumbling something about a person in her office, then she said fire and hand, then she collapsed."

By now, all the students from Mrs. Reigina's class have made their way to the hall, circling around to catch a glimpse. "Back to the classroom, all of you."

"This is ridiculous."

"What happened to her?" Another student wonders.

"Think she'll die?" The last student receives a dirty look from Mrs. Reigina as he walks back to class.

As it gets quiet, Mrs. Reigina looks over Mrs. Easegrom. "Guiney, get Mr. Testerman, quickly."

Guiney gets up and runs as fast as she can.

"Bethany, your phone, now! Support her head."

Bethany grabs the nurse's head as Mrs. Reigina stands and walks a few paces, out of earshot. Barely making out what she is saying, she does her best to listen to the conversation.

"No." Mrs. Reigina whispers. "I know what this means." There is a pause. "Fine!" She hangs up the phone and makes her way back to Mrs. Easegrom and kneels.

"Is the ambulance coming?"

"They are on their way. Stay here while I go see what is going on."

Mrs. Reigina leaves again, making her way to the nurse's office. As she vanishes around the corner, Guiney comes back with Mr. Testerman. It's not long before he too is on his knees checking her out.

"How long has she been like this, Guiney?"

"Maybe five minutes."

He pulls something out of his pocket. It's hard to see, but Guiney hears the small pop of a bottle being uncorked.

"What is it?"

"It's a wakening draft. Mrs. Easegrom created it some time ago. She has a way with herbs."

"Are you sure you should be doing that? Shouldn't we wait for help?"

"If we wait any longer, Bethany, she may not live long enough to need this."

The three of them sit, waiting, but for what? A few seconds pass before Mrs. Easegrom's back arches and a deep breath sucks back into her lungs.

"What happened? What am I doing here?"

"Mrs. Easegrom, do you not remember anything?"

"I remember being in my office, but I don't remember anything after ."

"Let's get her to her feet. Can you walk?"

"I think so."

Mr. Testerman helps her back to the office, while Guiney and Bethany begin their way to class.

"What was that?"

"No idea, Guiney, but I plan on finding out."

"Ninja mode?"

"Ninja mode."

Guiney and Bethany sit at the lunch table staring at their food. Neither one of them have spoken any more about the incident with Mrs. Easegrom. The silence is killing them, but neither want to speak first. Before long, neither will have to. Gabriel comes and sits next to Bethany.

Before he can ask what he wants to know, he notices there is some serious tension. Without wanting to cause any drama, he takes Bethany's hand and she looks up at him. "Hi."

"Hi."

"Hi to you too." Guiney snaps.

"Ok, I am not going to take offense, because there is clearly something going on. So, I'll go instead."

"It's nothing." Bethany breaks the tension and grabs his arm to stop him from leaving.

"Why do girls do that?"

"Do what?"

"Say it's nothing when it's clearly something."

"Listen, Gabriel, you are new to the Bethany/Guiney circle. You will learn sometimes nothing means nothing. Sometimes nothing means something, but we don't want to talk about it, got it?" Guiney goes back to picking at her food.

"Guiney?!"

"It's fine. I can see this is the nothing you don't want to be talking about. I came to see if you know what color you will be wearing to the dance so I can start looking for a vest and tie."

Her eyes beam as he talks about it, and her heart flutters at the thought of the two of them holding each other and making their way around the dance floor. "Bethany?"

She snaps out of her daydream. "Sorry, what were you saying?"

"The color of your dress?"

"Oh, sorry."

"Purple." Guiney pipes up.

Bethany looks at Guiney with the *'are you serious right now?'* look in her eyes. Guiney responds with a *'get with the program'* look of her own.

"Yes, purple."

"Right."

"Ok. We will talk more later about times and stuff; deal?"

"Deal."

"Until then." He takes Bethany's hand and kisses it before walking away.

She blushes slightly as she turns back to face Guiney. "Really?"

"What?" Guiney finally takes a bite of her food.

"I can answer for myself, you know."

"I am afraid you'd drool all over him before you got that far."

"Are you jealous?"

"Jealous? Of you and him? No. Jealous? Yes."

"Why?"

"Look at what you have."

"What do I have you don't?"

There is a moment of silence and neither says anything. Bethany waits for a response from Guiney, but all she gets is a shoulder shrug.

"If you are worried about losing my attention, don't. I have too much on my plate right now to worry about anything else. The dance will be the dance and nothing else."

"Are you sure?" Guiney raises her eyes, but not her head.

"Positive."

"I'll believe it when I see it."

"You really have such little faith in me you think I would desert you for a boy?"

"I don't believe you will do it on purpose, but things can happen."

"Wow, what a stab in the heart." Bethany thumps her chest with her fist.

"Don't be dramatic."

"I am going to. There is a reason why they call it best friends. You are the best part of me, and nothing will change."

"If you say so."

"Seriously, if you don't stop, I will smash this pie in your face." Bethany picks up a piece of apple pie.

"A threat?"

"Dare me?"

"Bring it on red." Guiney rises from her seat quickly and moves to the other side of the table.

With the pie in her hand, Bethany flings it at Guiney's face, missing by a few inches, landing on a student sitting behind her. Covering her mouth in shock, Bethany begins to apologize profusely while she gives the girl napkins to help clean it up. Luckily, only a little got in the girl's hair.

She raises herself from her seat, grabbing her own piece of pie and smashes it on Bethany's head, pressing the apples into the crevices of her hair.

"Oh dear." Guiney chimes in.

"You're even sweeter than you think you are now." The girl chuckles.

Everyone in the cafeteria waits to see what Bethany will do, but instead of getting angry, she takes a spoon full of mashed potatoes and flings it at the girl's face. The girl ducks in time and it flies over her shoulder and into the boy sitting next to her. He then gets up, and with a spoon full of peas, he flings it at Bethany. Doing her best to dodge it, the fight is on.

Thirty plus students fling food across the cafeteria at each other. Everyone is ducking, laughing, and having a good time. You can see the faculty trying to calm everyone down, but it's not working. It only makes the students laugh or try harder. One teacher even got a splat of something in her face.

It doesn't last long, though. As everyone is really getting into it, Mr. Testerman comes through the door as a tater tot hits him in the face. At least half the cafeteria gasps as silverware begins to drop to the tables and floor.

"I see we are having a bit of fun today, huh? Tell me, who is responsible for this?" His voice isn't angry, but you can tell he is serious.

No one moves while Bethany looks over at Guiney and mouths the words *'go big or go home right?'* So, standing on the table, she raises her eyebrows towards Mr. Testerman.

"Miss McAlester, I should have known. Follow me, please."

Making her way to his side, he ushers her out of the cafeteria, hearing the whispers behind her as the kids get back to their business of finishing their lunch. Before he leaves the doorway, Mr. Testerman turns to them, "All of you, clean up this mess."

Guiney stands in the doorway, watching Bethany walk the green mile.

As they walk toward his office, they pass a janitor filling a mop bucket in the closet. Mr. Testerman stops to say something to him, "You will need more than that, and I don't want you to lift a finger. You take all the cleaning supplies to the cafeteria. They are to clean it all. Stand watch, and if anyone tries to leave before it's finished, you let me know."

"Yes, sir."

They get about half way to his office before he finally says something to me, "This is not how I wanted our next conversation to be, Ms. McAlester."

"I started it between me and Guiney. I can't control what everyone else does."

"Nonetheless, you are the one who started it. Therefore, you are the one who will be taking the punishment."

"I know." She knew it was coming the moment she threw that piece of pie.

"First things first, you need to get cleaned up. Get to the locker room and take a shower. You smell like stale cafeteria food. Then, I want to see you in my office in twenty minutes. Got it, twenty minutes."

"Sir, yes, sir." She salutes him as she makes her way to the locker room.

Dancing under the water, she uses the shampoo bottle as a microphone. Belting out the words to Gangnam Style, she has no idea someone lurks in the shadows. The figure waits patiently, using the lockers as their hiding place, knowing to keep their breathing low so as to not be heard. They only move enough to stop from getting stiff while crouching behind one of the larger lockers. Steam from the hot shower covers the floor, creating an eerie feeling. The mix of heat from the steam and cold from the air give the figure chills while they wait for Bethany to walk towards the locker she keeps her clothes in. A slow creak of the hinges makes Bethany stop to listen.

"Hello?" No one answers. "Hello? Is someone there?"

Without responding, the stranger creeps around the wall of lockers, finding Bethany facing the opposite direction.

Her heart begins to beat faster, her eyes dilating in fear. "This isn't funny."

"What isn't funny dear?"

Her squeal is loud enough to echo through the whole locker room. "Don't do that."

"I am sorry. I didn't mean to startle you."

"You really shouldn't sneak up on people, Mrs. Easegrom."

"Was I sneaking, really? I didn't mean to, I swear."

Mrs. Easegrom's voice is low, almost to a high whisper. She does her best to hide her behavior, but the look on her face is not as easily hidden.

"What is it?"

"Mr. Testerman sent me to check on you to make sure you are alright. You have been a bit out of sorts lately, and he worries about his students."

"You can tell him I am fine, and I'll be there in a few minutes." Bethany turns away, doing her best to not change in front of the nurse.

"Oh no dear, I am waiting here for you. My instructions are clear." She sits down on the bench.

"Can you at least go somewhere else, so I can change?"

"If you wish." Mrs. Easegrom moves to the other side of the lockers.

"How are you feeling?"

"Oh, much better. Thank you for asking." Mrs. Easegrom begins to dig into a pouch she has at her side, pulling out a small vial of liquid and holding it in her hand.

"What happened yesterday?"

"I am not sure what you mean." Mrs. Easegrom makes her way back to the other side.

"You fainted yesterday, and you were covered in dirt and blood."

"Oh, it was nothing."

"It didn't seem like nothing."

"Don't worry your pretty little head about it. Come, let me see the scratch on your head."

Sitting on the bench, she uncorks the vial, causing Bethany to jump to her feet and knock the vial out of Easegrom's hand. It hits the floor, shattering the glass, liquid spilling around it. "I don't need any of your concoctions. I am fine."

She storms out of the locker room and makes her way to the principal's office.

Mrs. Easegrom takes it upon herself to follow out into the hallway. "Dear, I think you are forgetting something."

I turn to face her. "What?"

"Me." Mrs. Easegrom follows, accompanying Bethany to the principal's office.

When Bethany gets to the principal's office, Mr. Testerman is there waiting for her. He sits behind the desk with his fingers crossed and stares at the doorway. Picture when the president is making an address from the oval office, it's like that.

She stands there for a moment before entering the room completely, taking a seat in her favorite chair, and waits for her punishment. He doesn't speak at first, but stares. She can't tell what he is thinking or feeling by his expression.

"What."

He raises his hand to be quiet. "You don't get to speak. You know why you are here, and I know no matter what I say, you will continue to do whatever you want anyway. So, here's the deal, detention, but not any ordinary detention. Oh no, you will be cleaning the cafeteria with the ladies. Since you feel the need to make a mess, I feel the need for you to clean it. The students cleaned up their area, but the kitchen is not. I don't think it should be the responsibility of the cafeteria ladies to clean up your mess."

"My mess? I was not the only one doing it."

"No, but again, you are the one who started it."

She huffs, crossing her arms, and sitting back in the chair. "Fine."

"I am glad we agree, now off you go."

Mr. Fisher's class isn't as boring as most people would think a biology class would be. We have been working on the dissection of different fish. The smell is horrible, but the execution of it all is neat. We have gone through a few different types so far, and each time we do one, they continue to get bigger and bigger. At some point, he says we will be dissecting a baby shark. I am not sure how the girls will feel about it, but the boys are ready.

"Has everyone taken their spots? Good, now let's begin."

He steps to each of our tables, rolling a cooler on a cart, placing a fish on each of our lab tables. He has already laid out all the utensils we will need, and everything looks shiny and clean. You would never know we gutted other fish with them yesterday.

"Now class, here is how today's lesson will work. Each of you will answer one question. The person who gets the question correct will earn a reward. The reward will be the ability to step out of the actual cutting of the dissection process. If you guess incorrectly, you will be the one doing the cutting, pinning, and pulling. We will not be working in teams for the question portion, so you are on your own."

I look at Gwen, who is my partner in class. She smiles and turns back towards Mr. Fisher. I focus my eyes on her for a second before I turn to face him, not ready for what is coming. The dissecting I can handle, the questioning, not a chance.

"Let's begin with question one. Melvin, can you tell me what type of fish is in front of you?"

Melvin thinks for a minute before answering. He lowers and shakes his head no with a vague expression on his face.

His partner, Anna, raises her hand. Mr. Fisher waves it away and turns his attention to the next table. "Carmen, can you tell me what fish is in front of you?"

"It's a catfish, Mr. Fisher."

"Very good. You are free from dissection." He then looks at Melvin's partner. "Anna, what group do catfish coincide with?"

"No idea, sir." He shakes his head and moves on.

"Let's try this again. Melvin, what group do catfish coincide with?"

"I don't know." He still looks down.

Mr. Fisher shakes his head again and moves onto the next table. "Josh, can you tell me what group catfish coincide with?"

"Ray-finned, sir?"

"Very good, you are free from dissection. Now," he turns back to Anna, "try not to disappoint me. Tell me what the name of the item on the fish resembling a cat's whiskers is."

Anna's eyes light up, knowing the answer. "Barbels."

"Congratulations, you are free from dissection. Now, only a few more tables. So, as it stands, Melvin is the dissector and Anna is the examiner. James is the dissector, and Carmen is the examiner. Michael is the dissector, and Joshua is the examiner. Shall we continue?"

There are three tables left. Gwen and I are table one, Lyndsay and Donna are table two, and Cristine and Kristen are table three. We sporadically look back and forth at each other, hoping the other one will be the dissector.

"Gwendolyn, can you tell me what is the continent that doesn't house catfish in its waters?"

I look at her and I can see a bead of sweat roll down the side of her face. Does she not know it? She knows everything.

"You either? Alrighty then. Lyndsay, can you tell me what is the continent that doesn't house catfish in its waters?"

"Antarctica."

"Very good, you are free from dissection." There is a pause when he turns to Gwen and I again. A slight smirk makes its way across his face and I know he is coming for me. "Luthor, catfish exceed what length?"

I think for a minute. I don't know the answer, but I am not going to let him see that. I think back to some of the shows I watched as a kid. I am sure there has to be at least one that mentioned it. Nothing comes to mind, so I take a wild guess. "Eight feet?"

"Ding, ding, ding. Ladies and gentlemen, we have a winner."

"Really?" She whispers to me.

"It was a guess."

"Lucky guess."

"Last but not least, Cristine, can you tell me whether or not a catfish is dangerous to humans?"

"No, they are not. They make great eating too."

We all laugh, but it's broken when Mr. Fisher responds with a no.

"Incorrect. Kristen, are catfish harmful to humans?"

"Only some cases, sir. A few species have thorn-like scales behind their fins. They are not necessarily poisonous but can be hurtful."

"And we have another winner! Now we all know who the dissectors are and who the examiners are, so let's begin."

You can hear the rustling of everyone turning towards his or her fish. Gwen picks up its tail, crinkles her nose, and puts it back down again.

"Not bad."

"It smells horrible."

"It's a fish, it's not supposed to smell like roses."

She doesn't respond, but her glare is enough. She grabs a scalpel from the side of the board and clenches it in her right hand.

"Now, I want you to turn the fish, so its belly is facing you. Aprons on?"

"Check."

"Goggles ready?"

"Check."

"Scalpels on your mark?"

Gwen makes a small incision along the length of the fish's stomach. Before anything else, a strong odor comes pouring out. If you have ever been in a fish market on a hot day, you'll know the smell I am talking about. You can hear the gagging, coughing, and noises everyone is making.

"Let's open some windows, shall we?" Mr. Fisher suggests.

The smell doesn't really go away, but it becomes tolerable.

"Once you have made the long incision down its stomach. I want you to make two horizontal incisions along the top and bottom, forming an 'I' shape. As you are doing this. I will be coming around to see how well you know the outer working of our friend Tom here."

"Tom?"

"It's before your time, Lindsay. Tom and Jerry was a cartoon I used to watch growing up. Tom is a cat."

Mr. Fisher paces a bit before he goes table to table asking about the different parts of the outside of the fish. I can hear him asking two questions at each table. One is for the examiner and one for the dissector. When he finally gets to us, I put a brave face on. "And here we are at last. Miss Gwendolyn, can you show me where the caudal fin is?"

It takes Gwen a second, but she pulls the tail fin on the back of the fish. Mr. Fisher nods and turns to me. "Luthor, it's the moment of truth. Let's look at the inside. Can you tell me where the caudal peduncle is?"

"The what?"

"Caudal peduncle."

"Ah." I stare down the fish.

Something clicks in my mind as I think about what he asked Gwen. It's the same wording, just a different part. Therefore, if the caudal fin is its tail, then the caudal peduncle has to be close to it. I take a chance and point to the section between its middle fin and the tail fin.

"Close, but no cigar. The caudal peduncle runs the length of the fish vertically, almost like a spine."

He moves back to the front of the class and begins to write on the chalkboard. We all turn and look to see things a little more pronounceable.

As he finishes, he begins to give us our instructions. "Here is where we now stand. I want each of you to find these items inside the fish. You will then remove the items and place them on the card in front of you. The first team to remove all the parts and be correct will win a prize."

"What is the prize?"

"The bragging rights to the rest of the class and the knowledge you are smarter than you think; to work, James."

Gwen begins to pin the sides of the fish so we can easily see the inside. I know she wants to say something, but she is afraid to.

"What is it?"

"Nothing." She keeps her attention on Tom.

"Why do girls do that?"

"Do what?"

"Say nothing when clearly there is something."

"There are a lot of reasons."

"I'd love it if you would explain it to me."

"I wish I knew myself."

I don't want to push the issue, so I let it go. I look at the list on the board and write it down on the card in front of me. "Should we start with the heart?"

"Yeah, it's an easy one, it's right here." She pulls it with a pair of tweezers and removes it with the scalpel. "What's next?"

"Liver."

"Easy." She pulls again, placing it on the card. "Next."

"Spleen."

"Done, next."

"Pancreas." This one takes her a minute, but she is able to find it.

"Anything else?"

I look down at my list. "The rest says show, not pull."

"Fine." She has no emotion of substance. "We are ready, Mr. Fisher."

"Already? Wow, let's see what you have."

"The pulled stuff is here."

"Very good. Now can you show me where the ovary is?"

Gwen points to a long pink part of the fish, almost dead center of the belly.

"Very good. Show me the stomach."

"Here." I show him.

"Close, want to try again?"

I look at the fish for a minute, then point to a greenish-looking pouch right behind its gills.

"Now you've got it. Ok, last one for the win. Show me where the spinal cord is."

This one takes me a minute. I know the cord has to be long and thin, obviously. The problem comes when there are more than one long, thin cords. I play around inside the belly, pulling what looks like a vein out of the way. Behind it, I find a stiffer piece going all the way through its head, so that has to be it. I look up at Mr. Fisher and he nods.

I look at Gwen, hoping she will be happy we got them all right. The vacant expression hasn't changed, and it's worrying me. I nudge her shoulder, but she looks at me with sad eyes on the verge of tears. Before I can say anything, the bell rings and she bolts for the door.

I can't help but stand there for a minute, contemplating what could have changed so dramatically in the last few hours since breakfast.

"Way to go." Melvin's shoulder slams into my own as he walks by.

We make it to lunch and Gwen's mood hasn't changed. Knowing the person I am, I can't let it go. She sits there picking at her food, not even touching it to her mouth, and her color is getting paler than it was in biology. Her eyes are bloodshot, and you can tell she has finally let herself cry.

I curl up next to her and put my arm around her waist. She leans her head into my shoulder and I kiss the top of her forehead. "You are my best friend. I hate to see you like this. What is wrong?"

I can hear her taking in a few deep, broken breaths before she speaks. "I am worried."

"About what?"

"Everything. This has been too easy."

"What is easy?"

She slowly rises from my shoulder. "The house, school, whatever. I am worried about Bethany. I am worried about the status of our training, and mostly because it's been a little too quiet. Something isn't right."

"I know what you mean, but I think you are thinking too much into it. Think about what happened before. When we finished with Zeus, it was at least a month before anything else happened. Then came the Musketeers. Now we have a break, and I get to enjoy the quiet before another storm hits."

"I know, but."

"No buts, it will be fine."

"I highly doubt it, but I'll take your word for it."

She is a worrier, and in her own right, she is entitled to be. Her job as a guardian is as tough, if not tougher, than mine.

"We will get through this together. We have both proven there is nothing we can't handle."

She looks up at me and I can see the tears sitting in her eyes. She squints slightly as they make their way down her cheeks. I wipe them away, kiss her forehead again and ask her the most important question yet. "Can you help me with my homework?"

She punches me in the arm and we both break out into laughter. This is what friendship is about. This makes us who we are. We have the ability to take our fears, worries, and pain and make it better for each other. Our fear and worry will strengthen us; at least it's what I keep trying to tell myself. Is everything going to be ok? Are we going to get through this? These are things I have asked myself the last two times we have been called to do anything.

December 31st

Let's start off by saying that I am about over getting calls from the principal about Bethany's behavior. Dinner tonight will be interesting. Anyway, as many times as I have written in these journals, I realized I have not been truly

*honest with you or myself. Oh sure, I tell you about my day
and sometimes I tell you what's going on, but I never really
tell you how I am feeling deep down. I know these are
supposed to be for the future generations, but I think it's
important for them to know what it feels like as well as
what is happening. So, here it goes, it sucks; all of it. I hurt
every day, and I don't mean physically. There are days I
wake up mentally drained and I can't shake the funk. I have
been putting on a face for everyone and pretending I am ok,
but inside I am screaming. I can't really say what I am
screaming though; it would be inappropriate. Anyway, as
for the physical part, yes, my body hurts after an adventure
or after training for hours on end, but it's supposed to be a
good kind of pain, right? Whoever says pain is gain needs
to be tortured like this and see if they feel the same way.*

*I know you are all wondering, and yes, I still feel the same
way as I always have about Gwen. No, I am not going to do
anything about it. Everything is in her hands.*

*Now I am not done whining yet, so here is more. These
correspondence courses are going to be the death of me.
It's bad enough I have to do them, but to have two of them
on top of my regular classes, I am glad no one is calling on
me.*

*I am thankful I have a smart friend like Gwen. Whenever I
am stuck on anything, all I have to do is ask her and she
knows what it is or will be. The great part of a
correspondence course is I get to pick what I want to learn,
which makes it easier. I decided to go with American High
School for the company. They seem to be the most legit,*

although I really have no idea what it means to be accredited. I tried to find the two courses I know will benefit me the most.

It takes me some time, but I finally know what it will be. Health will help me diagnose a few minor things. The criminal justice class should help me gain some knowledge of the law enforcement side of things I may deal with. Now I have seventeen days to finish.

Let's add the rest of my classes in gym, sociology, science, creative writing, English, math, and history. A few, I get with no problems, the rest is another story. As usual, there are new teachers for history and gym, and they are as hard on me as the others were. I keep telling myself 'seventeen days, seventeen days', and eventually I will make it. In the meantime, it's dinner and homework.

I wonder what is being made tonight. Even with mom gone, it's nice to have someone who can cook in the house. I know Gwen means well when she tries, but the guardian is much better.

I'm over it!

As I sit here writing, I have been wondering over the last week if Gwen is right. Is the fact it has been so quiet a bad thing?

The dreams, or should I say nightmares, of my mother's death still haunt me nightly. Who knows how long it will take them to go away. This morning, Gwen had to wake me from my sleep because I was screaming and flailing around. I wish I could remember what part of my dream it was.

Bethany had her detention for the food fight she started. She told me about Mr. Testerman's rule of three strikes and you're out. It won't be the suspension she has to worry about if things don't change with her attitude. If she gets to where she gets kicked out of school or flunks out, she will be stripped of her powers.

Her guardian and I talked to her about it, and she seems concerned enough, but only time will tell if it's going to do her any good. I have to admit though, her attitude at home has been better; now we need to work on school.

So, Gwen and Bethany making breakfast together has become a thing now. I am not hungry, but I don't want to offend them since they take the time to make it all.

"Good morning, sleepy head."

"Blah."

"Will you ever be a morning person, Bethany?"

"Not likely."

"Pancakes?"

Bethany has a different look about her today. Her normal ponytail is now a curly do, and what used to be a plain face is now covered with makeup. There is a smell I don't recognize either. Is she wearing perfume?

"Who is he?"

"Who is who?"

"The reason you changed your look."

"Can't a girl change things up once in a while?" Gwen eyes Bethany with a slight smile.

I look at the two of them and know they are conspiring against me. Gwen knows who it is, and it will take some prying to get it out of her.

I eat my pancakes and speak no more of it. I have my ways of finding out who he is. It's my job as her brother to make sure any man other than me or her father deserves her. It's times like this I wish I had Gwen's ability to see things. In fact, now that I think of it, she hasn't gotten any visions from touching things in a while.

I look up at her across the table as she eats her eggs; scrambled well with shredded cheddar. I must have been looking at her for a while, because she slowly lowers her fork and lifts her eyes at the same time. Her expression changes from normal to creeped out.

"Why are you staring at me?"

"Daydreaming, sorry."

"Uh, huh."

"We are going to be late, come on." Bethany is already making her way to the front door.

We make it to school before the bell rings. On our way up the stairs, I can see Mr. Testerman standing there, nodding to Gwen and I as we walk past. We nod back and keep moving. Before we can get very far, the secretary comes out of the principal's office and ushers us in.

Mr. Testerman finally makes his way through the door, motioning his head for us to follow him into the office. He sits in the chair behind the desk and points for us to sit as well. There is a moment of silence as he intertwines his fingers and leans on the desk. He glances at us both, and the words following are not what I expected.

"It's good to see you, Luthor." His accent is a little heavier than I remember.

"Thank you?"

"You seem a little out of sorts. Is everything ok, Miss Merles?"

"A little confused is all."

"No need to be concerned."

"If I may, sir, where is Mr. Prendergast? He was the principal of the high school for the longest time. In fact, I saw him walking the halls yesterday."

"He has taken a leave of absence. I will be filling in at both schools until the end of the year."

"Seems like a heavy load, sir."

"Call me Mr. Testerman."

"Mr. Testerman."

There is another moment of silence and I can see his eyes are holding a heavy burden. The bags sitting under them are dark and the whites are filled with red veins. The man who originally stood tall and firm seems a little frailer to me.

"Why are we here?"

"Because I wanted you to be, Luthor."

"Do you need something from us?"

"Not per se."

"Is there something we can do?"

"Not exactly."

"Are you going to give us a clue as to what it is?"

"Here's the thing." He leans on the desk again. "I know."

"You know what?" Gwen gives him a mix of confusion and disbelief.

"I think the other shoe is about to drop." I lean in to her.

"I do wear a rather large size, Mr. McAlester, but there is no reason to insult my footwear."

"I don't mean."

"I know what you mean, and you are correct."

"What is this?"

Gwen and I rise from the chairs with the realization of what is happening.

"Oh no!"

Gwen places a hand on my arm, looking at Mr. Testerman. "Who are you?"

He stands before speaking. "My name is Tristan, Sir Tristan to be more precise."

"Tristan?"

"Yes, Sir Tristan, a Knight of the Round Table."

"Nope, not having it. You are not interrupting my last few days of school. I will finish, and no mission is going to change that." As I speak, I can feel the pull inside me. I double over, clutching my stomach. "Don't do this now."

I can hear Gwen yelling at him, but it fades till I can no longer hear them. With all my effort to resist, it's too late. I open my eyes to find myself on a dirt road, surrounded by chickens, vendors, and people I don't recognize. I let out my most aggravated yell when I hear a voice behind me.

"Now, now."

"Send me home!"

"In a moment." Tristan stands there with a proud smirk.

"How dare you?"

"Me, what did I do?"

"I told you no, and you brought me here anyway. Speaking of which, where is here?"

"Welcome to Camelot." He beams as he passes his arm across the street line.

"Oh, lord."

"Not quite, but we do have a king."

"I am not laughing. I am missing class right now and I am so close to graduating."

I do a slow turn to check out my surroundings as Tristan watches me take it all in.

"Magnificent isn't it?"

"It's perfect, can we go home now?"

"Wow, you really are the life of the party, aren't you?"

With a snap of his fingers, we are back in his office. My foot catches the edge of the chair and Gwen catches me as I topple over. It takes a moment to gain my footing, and I heave a little from the transportation between worlds.

"Are you ok?" She straightens me up.

"Feeling a little nauseous."

"Here, eat this, it will help." Mr. Testerman hands me a wrapped bar.

"Yes, Mr. Lupin."

"Who?"

"Nothing."

I open the wrapper and eat the granola bar. It's oats and honey, which is not exactly my favorite, but it will do. I continue to brush the crumbs off my shirt, trying my best to comprehend this new predicament.

"So, what is the problem?"

"We need your help."

"Obviously."

"The king has been missing for some time. The lady has as well. With the threats looming, we need them." His eyes plead with me. You can see the strain this mission is putting on him.

"How many others are there?"

"What do you mean?" .

"How many more of you are there?"

"Six." He begins to count on his fingers.

"Who are they?" Gwen looks in his direction and he can see she is not impressed.

"Merlin, Guinevak, Lancelot, another Knight of the."

"I know who he is."

"Then there are Gawain, Lady Ragnall, and myself"

"Are you sure there are no more?"

"Yes."

Gwen grips the arm of the chair and the muscles in her arms tense up. The color in her face goes from pale freckle to red hot, as she slowly begins to rise, and her legs shake.

"Who is at the junior high and who is at the high school?"

There is fear in Mr. Testerman's eyes as she stands fully. Can it be that he is afraid of Gwen?

"Young guardian, please understand, we mean no harm here."

"Then leave."

"Gwen?"

"I've heard enough, Luthor. He, nor anyone else, will stand in my way. I have 10 days left. If they want my help, they can wait until then."

She walks out the door, leaving Mr. Testerman, I mean Tristan stunned. I was normally the one losing my temper, but she beat me to it.

Lunch is quiet. Gwen has spent most of the time picking at her food, while keeping her head down. I am sitting across from her and doing my best to make conversation, but all I get are grunts and moans. I keep trying to get her to look up, but she won't. I decide since she won't talk to me about what is going on, I will write instead.

January 8th cont.

This morning was a handful for sure. Mr. Testerman is now one of the people I need to look out for. When he came to us with the news he is a Knight of the Round Table, I thought instantly they were going to do their best to get me to help them right away. After Gwen's outburst in his office, she hasn't been the same. Is the stress of it all getting to be too much for her? Has she been putting on a good front this whole time?

As a guy, I am oblivious to things like this. Girls are as confusing as the constellations. I keep asking myself questions repeatedly, trying to figure out whether or not to push the issue. Normally I would, but this time seems different. This time seems more intense.

Well, the bell is about to ring. I want to make sure she gets to class. Looking at her, my heart is breaking. What can I do for her?

Here we are, History. Mrs. Granada is another teacher looking younger than her years. I would put her at twenty-two or twenty-three, maybe, a newbie in the art of teaching. She definitely has her wits about her though. She isn't taking any crap from the students.

"Good afternoon class. I hope you all enjoyed your lunch. Today we will be doing things a little different. I want you to open your books to page forty-two."

I can hear a snicker from one of the students in the background. A few of us turn, but whoever did it doesn't make themselves known.

"Mrs. Granada?"

"Yes, Melvin?"

"What is the answer to life, the universe and everything?" He giggles slightly at his question.

"Forty-Two."

Melvin and a few other students cheer. I am not sure why, but to them the number forty-two is significant. The only thing I know the number to be significant to is Jackie Robinson.

"Alright, alright, calm down."

Turning back to the board, she begins to write again, starting with a few verses from the bible. I watch as stroke by stroke, the specs of chalk float through the air. As they make their way across the classroom, the light coming through the windows catches it. The swirling pattern caused by the slight breeze allows the chalk dust to dance in the air. I am lost in the movement of it all when I hear a slam bringing me out of my trance. I look up and notice Gwen is gone, Mrs. Granada looks upset, and the class is in awe. A younger kid stands near the doorway with a pass in his hand. I've never seen him before, but there are many kids at this school I don't know.

"You may go, Andrew. Thank you for delivering the message."

I know I was not completely out of it. How did I not hear anything happen? Mrs. Granada stands there for a few moments until she takes a deep breath, lowers her arm, and turns her attention back to the board. There are now three bible verses up there. Underneath them, there are instructions on what we are to do with them. You can tell whatever transpired made an impact. Her writing becomes sloppier, and she is writing slower than usual. My mind drifts to the redheaded love of my life, who is somewhere fuming with anger.

"I want you all to follow these instructions carefully. There will be points docked for any step you don't complete correctly. Good Luck! You have twenty minutes."

The first verse on the board is *'Isaiah 40:29-He gives strength to the weary and increases the power of the weak.'* The assignment is to rewrite the verse so it's more modern, and then explain what we think it means, and lastly, write a one-paragraph story with it. I was never a good writer, so as the clock ticks louder and louder in my ear, I become more and more flustered.

I continue onto the second verse; *'I Corinthians I 6:13- Be on your guard; stand firm in the faith; be courageous;*

be strong.' The third one is *'Proverbs 15:20- A wise son brings joy to his father, but a foolish man despises his mother'*. The longer I look at the verses, the blurrier the page gets. Lifting my head, I peek at the clock to see how much time I have left. If my calculations are correct, I have now wasted ten minutes staring into the abyss of my inability.

I sit up straight, focus my eyes, and do what any good student would, fake it till I make it. Verse number one, let's see. He gives strength to the weary and increases the power of the weak. Rewritten in modern terms? Ugh. Let's go with this, 'If you are tired, he will strengthen you. If you are wimpy, he will make you superman.' This is easier than I thought.

Ok, next one. 'Be on your guard; stand firm in the faith; be courageous; be strong.' Let's say, 'You need to be smart, proud, careful, and stealthy.' Ok, last one: 'A wise son brings joy to his father, but a foolish man despises his mother.' This one might be a little tougher. 'If you are smart, you can make your father a happy man, but if you are a moron, you won't have your mother's love.'

Now I have to figure out what it means, oh lord, my mind is not made for this. Ok, breathe, and go. Verse one means God will be able to give you the strength you need and never let you become weak. Verse two means you need to be careful you don't do things to disappoint your family. No wait, that's verse three, dang it. Ok, verse two means you need to watch your back and stay ninja. Now verse three is the not to disappoint family.

I look up at the clock again and realize I only have four minutes left to write three paragraphs. I scribble away with whatever gibberish I can think of. I move my hand frantically, praying she will be able to understand my writing.

The bell rings as I am putting the last period on paper. "Bring them to me on your way out."

Leaving class, I make my way through the hallway and I pass Gwen's locker. She isn't there, but she must have been. It's not shut all the way, and I can see a small piece of paper sticking out. I reach for it, unfold it, and read what is written. The wording is sloppy, but the words are clear enough; 'we should talk' and it's signed by Mr. T.

Is this the message Andrew delivered? Is Gwen in the office with Mr. T. now? I want to ditch class and find out for myself, but I know everything I do from here on out will impact me graduating early.

So here Gwen sits, waiting patiently in the principal's office for Mr. Testerman to be done with whoever is in there with him. What can he possibly want me to know about?

I can hear the rustling of chairs moving, and I do my best to keep a civil face as a student I don't know comes through the door. Mr. Testerman follows behind but doesn't acknowledge me until after the student has left.

As he begins his way towards his office. I stand to block his path. "What?"

"Please lose the attitude, Ms. Merles. Whether or not you like who I am, I am still your principal and I do have the authority to take action against unruly teenagers." He snaps back, making his way around me and into the office.

He gets back to his desk, leans back in his chair, puts his feet up, and places his hands behind his head.

"Comfy?"

"Quite. Now to the business at hand; sit."

"I'll stand, thanks." She places her hands on the back of the chair to steady her nerves.

"I have spoken with some of the others, and they have agreed we will wait until after you and Luthor finish your schooling. As of January twenty-third, I hope you decide to join us in our quest." He lowers his feet to the ground and stands for a moment, pacing back and forth behind his chair. With each pass, he looks at her briefly, but says nothing.

"Enough!"

Mr. Testerman stops and looks at her, their eyes meet, and a genuine feeling of disgust comes over her. "Ms. Merles, I will remind you again, and for the last time I am still your principal. Whatever is going on with you right now to cause such disobedience will cease."

"You would really suspend me or give me a detention? You need us. Are you going to risk it?"

"Would you like to see? I hate to tell you Ms. Merles, but the reason we are here for your help is more for Luthor's benefit than our own. This mission will decide his fate far more than the last two he has done. Now I ask you, are you willing to risk it?"

He sits back down in his chair and waits for a response. Did someone finally break her? She can feel her hands shaking and legs buckling from the weight of it all as she makes it to the front of the chair before finally collapsing into it.

"I don't know what is happening to me. This person I am becoming, is not who I am."

"There is a reason."

"What is the reason?"

"I am glad you are sitting down for this part."

So, what about the trials?

January 9th

So, Mr. Testerman is Tristan, a knight in Camelot. Surprise! I was able to meet with him after Gwen left, and he told me the same thing he told her. This mission, if I choose to accept it, is more to my benefit than theirs. He didn't explain why, so I left it as is for now.

My conclusion as of now is this; Mrs. Reigina and Mr. Fisher must be someone different too. There is something a little off about them. Didn't you find it funny? Tristan introduces himself and suddenly Mrs. Reigina is leaving, and Mr. Fisher with the "playing coy" bit about the pass. Something seems a little fishy. Get it? Fishy? Ok, I think it's funny.

One of the things I did get from Gwen is the discussion she had with Mr. Testerman about why she is acting the way she is. He explained there is a part of the path a guardian takes where they are made to overcome specific emotional struggles. How does he even know about them? Her plan is to speak with Bethany's guardian about it. My guess is, the strain of it all is getting to be too much for her and she is about to break.

I am now down to twelve days left of school. If you want to get technical, I only have eight days left, if you take out the weekends. Two weeks. I can make it two more weeks.

As of right now, I am ready to take the correspondence test for the criminal justice class. I made it through the practice tests at the end of each chapter and have reviewed all the questions. The test itself is like twenty questions, so if I get any wrong, I can fail it easily enough.

I may have Gwen or Bethany test me with the questions before I take it. At least this way I can know whether I'd be close to the right answer or not. For now, I plan on enjoying the rest of the evening.

The three of us, plus Bethany's guardian, are going to take a trip to the zoo, and then maybe to the park where we spent so much time with the gods. It will be nice to go back and reminisce about the good times on the journey.

With all this writing I have been doing recently, I don't think I ever really said what Bethany's guardian's name is. In fact, I am not sure I even know what her name is.

Well, I must go! I smell dinner.

As I head toward the kitchen, I can see a figure who normally isn't there around this time of night. Bethany's guardian is standing over the sink doing something, Gwen is sitting on the couch reading, and Bethany is nowhere to be seen.

I stand in the doorway for a few seconds before entering the front room. I don't want to startle Gwen and have her go all "snapped" on me. She is always oblivious to her surroundings when she is engrossed in one of her books.

I creep slowly, trying not to disturb her. As I get closer, she slams the book closed and I jump. She doesn't turn around, but she speaks. Her tone is calm, although there is a bit of sarcasm and irritation to it. "You know I can hear you, right?"

She finally turns and I stand there, not wanting to move for fear of my life. "I didn't want to disturb you."

"It's fine." She opens the book back up and continues her reading.

I make my way to the other side of the couch and lay down on my back, putting my head in her lap. She glances down at me briefly but doesn't say anything. I give her a few more moments before I speak again, "Will you ask her tonight?"

She doesn't respond.

"About the trials."

Still nothing.

"The ones Mr. Testerman mentioned."

Nada.

"Can we dance the waltz like Ginger Rogers and Fred Astaire?" I laugh slightly but stop as soon as I feel the book hit the top of my head.

"You're not funny." She stands up and lets my head hit the cushion with a nice thump.

I swing my feet to the floor and stand up, taking a few steps forward. Her back is turned, and I wrap my arms around her from behind to hold her for as long as she will let me.

I can hear and feel her exhale a deep breath. My first thought is she is going to pull away, but she crosses her arms over mine and lays her head back on my shoulder. Turning it slightly, she whispers, "thank you".

"Anytime."

"Can we get a room, please?"

"Way to ruin the moment, dragon's dung."

"Bite me, lizard breath."

"What have you been up to?" I reach in to give Bethany an unwanted hug.

"Homework, can you let go now, I can't breathe!"

"My bad." I raise my hands in surrender.

She gets in a good jab to the stomach and plops down on the side chair. "I have a random thought."

"And what pray tell may it be?"

Gwen makes her way to the other side of the couch, heading towards the kitchen stopping at Bethany's next words. "We should call Joe."

"Joe, as in mom's Joe? Joe we haven't seen since we told him about mom, Joe?"

"Is there another Joe we know?"

"Hey you rhymed!"

"Shut up, troll snot."

"Trying to keep the mood light." I slide backwards off the arm of the couch and lay back with my feet dangling over the edge.

"Yes, Joe."

"What made you think of him?"

"I don't know. I was lying there thinking about stuff and he came to mind. Then I got to thinking about his reaction to all of this and my heart breaks for him. I mean, come on, I know mom didn't really tell us about him, but the more I think about it the more I feel like we owe him more than we give him."

When did my little sister get so smart and sentimental?

"He is a nice guy, and you can tell whatever he felt for mom was genuine." Gwen makes her way to sit by me. She lifts my head and places it back on her lap.

"I think we should call him. I want to invite him over for dinner. I want to at least make sure he is doing ok." I can tell Bethany is trying to tug at our heartstrings, and she is succeeding.

"So, say we all."

"You know, Luthor, these nerdy references of yours are getting to be ridiculous."

"Never knock the nerdom, Bethany, for it is we who rule the world, muahahaha."

"Your highness, dinner is ready."

You can hear Gwen and Bethany snicker and we start to get up and make our way to the kitchen. "I am not laughing."

"We are."

"As for Joseph, I will call him in the morning and find a time when he is free." Mentions the guardian.

"No, I want to do it."

"So be it, Bethany, I will leave you now."

"Won't you join us?" Gwen places a hand on her shoulder. "It will be a nice change."

"I appreciate the offer, but maybe another time."

"Wait! I have something I need to speak with you about."

"When you have finished your dinner, come and see me."

Gwen stands there motionless for a few seconds. Her shoulders slumped and her back arched. There is a look of defeat in her eyes.

"Don't." I tell her.

"Don't what?"

"There is time, so come and eat. If you want, I'll go with you and we can talk to her together."

"Come on, let's eat, I am starving."

"Patience, young padawan."

"I am so over you, brother."

We each take our normal seats at the table and observe the meal in front of us. I go first and start spooning some green beans onto my plate. They weren't with almonds like mom used to make, but I would not expect her to know.

You can smell the pork loin, and see the chunks of crushed pineapple she used to glaze the top of it. It makes me wish I was around a bonfire and there is a pig roasting on a spit. I slice it before I realize Gwen is tearing up again. I drop the knife and turn to her.

As I reach for her, she pushes my hand away and shakes her head. "I am fine."

I know she isn't, but I know there is nothing I can really do for her right now. I try to change the subject as best I can. "How big of a piece do you want?"

She looks at me as if I should know better, so I cut her a piece a few inches thick and drop it onto her plate. There is a little juice at the bottom of the pan, so I scoop it up and drizzle it over the meat. Then I do the same for Bethany and myself.

I look over at Bethany as I plate her food. "Ya good?"

"I'm good."

"Good."

Once the last plates are put away, I wipe my hands and we are ready to go talk to the guardian.

I take Gwen's hand and she turns towards me. "Deep breath, young guardian"

"Deep breath, and don't ever call me that."

"Let's go."

I guide her out the door and up the stairs. With each creak of the wood, I can feel her grip getting tighter and tighter. I stop about halfway up and turn to her. "No matter what she says, remember what I told you; you and me."

We reach her floor and I knock lightly like I always do. There is a faint voice calling to come in as I turn the knob on the door. The room is dimly lit, and the furniture has been moved around. I haven't thought about it much, but things seem a lot different since Grams died. There are fewer pictures on the walls. The knick-knacks are gone, the furniture has been reupholstered, and it's a lot cleaner than it used to be too. There isn't as much dust floating through the air and collecting on all the things Grams had sitting around. God, I miss her. I give Gwen's hand a squeeze and we move to the couch.

Before we can sit down, the guardian comes out from the hallway and stops. "Come with me." She turns back and makes her way back down the hallway.

I can see the light on in the study, and the last time I was in the room, Grams was getting us ready for our first mission. She never did get the picture of us, and like the rest of the apartment, the room has been cleaned and organized. The pictures still hang on the wall, and the boxes containing the ashes of Gwen's family rest on the bookshelf. It makes me think of my mother, lying there alone, knowing I need to take the time this weekend to see her.

The guardian stands at the bookshelf and runs her fingers along the line of old leather-bound books. "It's here somewhere."

"What is?" Gwen moves toward her.

"The answer to your questions."

"How do you know what my questions are?"

"It's my job to know. Plus, it's time."

"Time for what?" Gwen grabs the guardian's arm and turns her.

"We are sisters, and for that reason I will not take offense to this action. Listen carefully, because what I have to say will mean a great deal. For one moment, if I see you falter in your strength I will take the steps to see it doesn't happen again." The guardian pulls her arm from Gwen's grasp and turns back towards the bookshelf.

Gwen cowers her way to the armchair in the corner. Running her fingers through her hair, she pulls it back into a ponytail, sits back, and crosses her legs. Keeping her back straight, and her body firm, she waits and says nothing. I keep looking back and forth between them, waiting for one of them to say something, anything.

Minutes pass before the guardian finally speaks. "Here it is."

Gwen jumps to her feet and stands as close as a shadow. She attempts to peek over the guardian's shoulder, but she is much taller than Gwen. The guardian peers down at her through the tip of her nose and waits there until Gwen is finished bouncing on the balls of her feet.

"This book contains the information you will need to complete three tasks. Each task will guide you to the path you are meant to take. You need to be cunning, vigilant, obedient, and willful. These things will allow you to make it through. Not to mention the need to be wise and compassionate."

"That's all?" Gwen turns away, making her way back to the armchair in the corner.

"Trust me when I say I have faith in you. You have made it this far and have come out victorious. These three trials will only bring you closer to being a guardian of the highest standing."

"I see."

"She is right. You have done a lot already, and as of right now, you are ahead of the game." I'm hoping my words of encouragement will get her back to her feet. "You have done more at your age than some people will do in a lifetime."

She gives me a flat-lipped smile and looks up at the guardian. "Where do I begin?"

"I will hand you the book. I will let you know what chapters you will need to look at first. Hold tight to it, it will be a lifeline for you. For now, put your fears aside, we shall enjoy this evening. Are you ready?"

Gwen looks at me, and I give her a reassuring glance. She puts the book under her arm and takes my hand as we make our way to the door. The guardian closes the door to the study and ushers us out of the apartment and down the stairs.

Bethany meets us at the door as she hands me my wallet, and Gwen her purse. The Guardian clears her throat to signal something, but none of us know what.

I look up at her and without really knowing how, she speaks to me. *Your weapons.* "Seriously?"

"Seriously."

I go back to the apartment and grab the sword, Gwen's bow, and Bethany's staffs. When I make it back to the hallway, they are already outside waiting for me. I have never seen it before, but the guardian is laughing, and the other two are sitting there with their arms crossed, doing their best not to.

I stand in the doorway with all the weaponry haphazardly hanging from my arms. I wonder what is so funny until I realize the reason. I went for the weapons when I didn't have to. All I have to do is call for them when we get to where we are going.

"I hate all of you." I can hear their laughter grow as I turn back to the apartment to drop the weapons off.

We make it to the zoo and pay to get in. I haven't been here since we helped Zeus defeat Hera and it feels weird. Not that much time has passed, but it feels like so long ago. What has it been, like six months or something?

I stare at the food cart, hoping Dionysus will pop his head out of the window, but he doesn't. I look off in the distance to the dolphin exhibit, tempted to go in and see if Poseidon will answer. I glance over and Gwen knows what I am thinking without even having to say it.

The guardian looks at both of us and drops her shoulders in defeat. "Fine."

Gwen and I take off running, while the guardian and Bethany slowly make their way. We get to the doors, each of us taking a handle. Stopping for a minute, we look at each other once more before making sure. "Ready?"

"Ready."

We swing the doors open and make our way into the exhibit. There are a lot more people here than last time, and the noise echoes through the glass building. Gwen and I walk up to the edge of the water and watch our reflections.

"You do it." She pushes.

"Are you sure?" I feel a wave of excitement wash over me. The hairs on my arms and neck stand on end as the nerves settle into my stomach. "Here it goes."

Before I can say anything, everything stops. Gwen and I see everyone frozen in time, while a dolphin halfway out of the water rests in mid-air, the trainer's arm raised in command. As we make a full circle, I can see Bethany and the guardian coming toward us.

"Well, this is interesting."

"What's happening?"

"I have no idea, Bethany, but I'm sure we are about to find out."

Within seconds, I can feel something wet hit the back of my head. I turn and get a face full of water. Wiping it off, I can hear the others laughing at me. When I am able to regain focus, I can see what caused them to think it was so funny. Poseidon is raising a wave out of the water, and it's making its way toward us. The girls squeal as the water drops from above, soaking us from head to toe.

Poseidon's laugh fills the place with such energy and warmth. "I haven't done that in ages."

"Hilarious." I begin wringing out my shirt.

"How are you, young traveler? Oh, and Gwen, my dear, you look amazing as always."

"Thank you, Lord Poseidon."

"And who are these two fine creatures?"

Bethany and the guardian make their way towards him. The guardian bows before introducing herself, "My Lord, I am Angelic, High Guardian."

"It's a pleasure to meet you, Lady Angelic." He bows.

"The lady is unnecessary, you can call me Angelic."

"And you?" He looks toward Bethany.

She stands there with an astonished look on her face. Other than the guardians, she hasn't been exposed to too much else in this world. Gwen and I flank her, and then slowly walk her forward. "This is my sister, Bethany."

"I can see the resemblance. It's a pleasure to meet you as well, Miss Bethany." He bows in her direction.

"Thank you." She gives an awkward curtsey.

"She's a cute one, Luthor. Is she as stubborn as you?"

"You have no idea."

I feel a sting in my arm and turn to find Bethany's expression of disappointment and frustration. Her lips are tight, and her cheeks are flush. "Seriously?"

"Well, I am not going to lie to a god."

"You are impossible." She storms off in the opposite direction and sits on the bleachers.

I turn back towards Poseidon, and you can see he is enjoying this. "I see what you mean. What can I do for you, young guardian?"

"Nothing."

"Nothing?"

"Nothing."

"Well." He pouts slightly.

"We wanted to see you."

"Well, that's different then. It's good to see you."

"Are you well? How are the others?"

"All is well. Hera is still behaving; which is a shock to us all." He twists the gold cuff sitting on his wrist.

"Is something wrong?"

"Oh no, my lady, just a little sore. As good as it's to see you, I must go. I wish you well, young traveler, and you, my radiant guardian." He smiles as he makes his way backwards.

"Poseidon!"

"Yes?"

"Tell the others I miss them as well."

Everything begins to slowly get back to normal. Bethany makes her way back towards us as we venture toward the exit. Her face is somber, and I know what I said hurt her feelings. Normally I would try to console her, but at this point she will have to toughen up, like I did. If everyone keeps babying her, she won't get any stronger.

"Earth to blockhead!"

I look at Bethany. "Yes, madam butt munch."

"One of the worst insults you have ever thrown. Come on, we are going to walk around."

"Yes, ma'am."

We walk for a while and end up at a gazebo short of the birdcages. My mind drifts again as I think about Aphrodite. As we sit, every memory from the first adventure comes flooding back to me.

I am happy things are going well, but I am concerned about the way Poseidon messed with the cuff on his wrist. I am sure there is more he isn't telling me. Alas, something to look into at another time.

It's not the same as I wait for the peacock, Bennu, or something to come at me, but nothing ever does. I know I should be ok with it, but a part of me misses it the longer we are here.

The adventure in France was exciting and everything, but there was something about Olympus that's still sticking with me. I think it hit me more. Maybe it was because it was my first one, or maybe it was because of my father. Maybe it was because I grew so close to them, and I didn't have the closeness as much in France.

Deep in thought, I don't realize I am being snuck up on until something hits me hard on my butt. I turn around and find Gwen laughing hysterically.

"You really want to go?"

"Bring it on blockhead."

"I am laughing on the inside." She has already changed into her 'new' attire. Her tight black leggings, long boots, and waist cincher gives her a shape making my heart skip a beat, or two.

"You're staring again." She takes a fighting stance.

"Sorry." I turn away and chant the words so I can change myself. "Out of time my sword shall find, the way to me, so I may bind."

The light grows around me, and I can feel the tingle running through my skin. As I always do, I look down to watch the change happen, starting with my boots, then my knickers, and finally my shirt and vest. I place a hand on the hilt of my sword as I look to make sure no one is watching. We are in the clear, and I can hear Bethany and Angelic already going at it.

"You are wasting time, young traveler."

"Are you ready to be pummeled?"

"You wish."

We spar as we have throughout the last few months. I lunge, she ducks, and our swords meet somewhere in the middle, while the clank of metal can be heard for miles. As we continue, people gather around us as though we are some kind of show. Gwen and I stop for a minute to catch our breath, while Bethany and Angelic keep going.

We look at each other, then look at the people gathering around us, the crowd growing larger and larger. There are a few cheers, and a few words of motivation from different spots. I wink at Gwen and we take our stance. As we do, a roar grows from the people gathered there. I smile and something in my heart explodes with excitement.

I make the first move, go straight for her abdomen, and you can hear them gasp. She turns in enough time to dodge the attempt, when her sword catches mine and a spark flies. With each passing strike, you can hear the oohs and ahhs of the crowd. Every once in a while, they cheer us on.

After an hour or so, we stop, raise our swords in front of us, lower them, then bow to each other. I have never heard a group of people grow so loud in, well, ever. We turn to the crowd and make another bow. Then the crowd slowly begins to disperse, while Bethany and Angelic join us.

"Ego much?"

"All in good fun, sis."

"Uh huh." She snickers and makes her way to the bench across the grass.

"Very brave, and stupid." Angelic joins Bethany.

"What?"

"Nothing?" Angelic's look is disappointing.

"Fine, who's hungry?

All three women raise their hands, so we make our way to a cart nearby to grab some snacks. I decide to go with ice cream since, well, it's ice cream. They make these blizzard things like Dairy Queen; Oreo and M&M with chocolate ice cream and chocolate syrup, yummy. Bethany decides on some kettle corn, but I think I have a love/hate relationship with kettle corn. I love the taste but hate when the hull is stuck in my teeth. Gwen decides on cotton candy, and I always wonder if the colors really are different flavors. Out of all the ones I have tried over the years, they all seem to taste the same to me. Last but not least, Angelic goes with the ever-basic bag of peanuts. No honey roasted, no candied, no salt.

I can hear her whisper something, but I can't make it out. I stop long enough to listen, and when she realizes Bethany and Gwen are too, she stops, looks at us while slightly embarrassed, and lowers her head.

"Don't."

Her eyes are soft, softer than they have ever been. She gives me a slight smile and blinks a few times, shyly. "I have always needed to be strong. Every so often, I like to be weak."

"We all do." I reach for her shoulder.

"Everyone has their moments." Gwen chimes in. "We are only so strong. It's ok to be weak sometimes. When you are, or when you need to be, you have us."

"Thank you, but I am better now. I have been away from my family longer than I have been before, and I miss them dearly." Angelic wipes a tear away with the tip of her finger.

"Tell us about them." Gwen scoots closer to her, cotton candy in hand, ready for a story.

"Well, I have two brothers and two sisters, and I am the second oldest. I also have three nieces and four nephews."

"What are their names?"

"My siblings?"

"Yeah."

"Christina, Steven, Diana, and Michael."

"They are guardians as well?"

"Correct, but my oldest sister didn't marry a fellow guardian, so he is in for a bit of a shock when he finds out."

"Kind of like Joe."

"Like Joe." Bethany whispers as she pulls her phone from her back pocket and swings one leg over the bench to stand. I can tell she is dialing as she makes her way farther and farther from us. She is calling him, and she wanted to do this on her own, so I let her.

"You are daydreaming again." Gwen punches my shoulder.

"For the love." I rub my arm.

"Lightweight."

I look up and realize Angelic has left and is standing by Bethany. Gwen and I watch the moments unfold second by second. Bethany stands with her back to us while her phone rests on her ear. Angelic stands at her side, tall and proud; her protector. It's not long before the phone comes down, the body turns, and the guardian protects.

Gwen and I get ourselves up and make our way towards them. I can hear the crying far enough away to know whatever was said in the conversation is not good. I wrap my arms around her from behind, and Gwen stands by her side. Angelic doesn't join in, but I can tell she wants to. She clears her throat and gazes to find people staring again. This time it's not to applaud us.

"We should go."

"No, I am fine. I want to hear more about Angelic's family."

"Are you sure?" Gwen rests a hand on Bethany's shoulder. "Do you want to talk about what happened?"

"Not right now."

"Whatever you want." Gwen puts her arm around Bethany's waist and guides her back to the benches, while Angelic and I follow, keeping a bit of a distance.

Back at the benches, we sit and listen intently while Angelic finishes telling us about her family. "Where was I?"

"You, brothers, and sisters." Bethany's demeanor hasn't changed and it worries me.

"Right, my brothers and sisters. My older sister married outside of the guardian circle. It was against the wishes of our parents, but she is a strong-willed person. She gave me four beautiful nieces and nephews, and they are all old enough now, except for the youngest one. He's not quite there yet to even consider the choice of guardianship."

"You said you have six."

"Correct, Bethany. I have another niece and another nephew. They, as well, are too young to be considered."

"Will you ever have kids?"

A sudden sadness reaches Angelic's face. Looking closely, you can see the tears forming under her eyelids. She blinks a few times and wipes another tear away. "No, Gwen."

"Why not?"

"It's not an option for me. Now, please leave the matter be."

Gwen's shoulders slump, and her head lowers. "I am sorry."

"It's fine. The news of this being was a long time ago. Does it still hurt? Yes. Will it ever change? No. Have I learned to deal with it? I have to."

"Have you ever considered adopting?"

"With what I do, Miss Bethany, maybe it's best I don't. My sister is no longer a full guardian, so it's easier for her to have children. As I have said, I am ok with it now." She stands up briefly "We should get going. The zoo will close soon, and you need your rest."

"Angelic? Will you consider me like a daughter?"

Angelic doesn't answer Bethany in words. Instead, she embraces her with open arms instead. "I can never replace your mother."

"Oh, I know, but I want you to know you will always have me."

"Nothing would make me happier than to consider you as family."

"Then so it is."

"As long as you don't call me mom."

"Deal."

Who's T.K.?

Gwen sits with the book in her lap, running her fingers over the leather-bound cover, watching a droplet of water hit the spine. There is a moment when she wants to throw the book across the room and never open it. Instead, she lets the battle rage in her mind, but not in the open.

Lifting the cover, she finds a hand-written note in the top corner of the page. It's faded, but legible enough to read. *'This book belongs to you, the one who will follow in the steps of those who came before you.'* It's signed with the initials. *T.K.* Turning to the first page, she begins reading about the beginning of her journey. *This book is not for the faint-hearted, nor is it for the weak minded. The trials residing in the pages of this book are made to test your mind, your strength, and your will. You will not know when said trials will occur, but these words here will help guide you for when the time comes.*

At no time should you rely on the contents of this book for survival alone. You must take these words and combine them with your own knowledge of the world around you.

With each person this book is passed to, it's the responsibility of the guardian to write his or her trials to prepare the next generation. You, as well as those to follow you, will learn of the trials of previous guardians, them as people, their powers, and what you wish them to know. In my trials, I discovered the ability to heal. I shall tell you more later.

Before you begin, note one last thing, these trials are for you and you alone. No one and nothing will be there to guide you other than this book and your own skills.

"So, who is T.K.?"

There is a knock at the door, startling her. A low creaking fills the room as the door opens slowly. Bethany sticks her head in to make herself known. "Ya busy?"

"No, come on in." Gwen pats the bed. "What's on your mind?"

"Well." Bethany begins to tear up.

She wraps her arms around Bethany as she sits next to her. "Whenever you are ready."

With a sniffle, Bethany begins what she came in to say. "So, the phone call with Joe."

"Ah yes, Joe."

"What is that supposed to mean?" Bethany snaps.

"Easy!"

"Sorry." She lowers her head. "When I called Joe, he answered right away. I let him know who I was and explained we were thinking of him and wanted to check in on him."

"What did he say?"

Bethany breaks down and lays herself in Gwen's lap. She reaches for the box of Kleenex on the nightstand and pulls a few out. She gently wipes away Bethany's tears and hands her another for her nose. In between the heaves for breath, Bethany speaks again.

"He. Said. To go. To hell."

"Are you serious?"

Bethany sits back upright and blows her nose. She begins to slow her breathing and calm herself down. Before she speaks again, she gives her nose another blow, tossing the wrinkled-up Kleenex towards the small pink garbage can in the corner but misses. "Figures."

"I'll get it." Gwen gets up and throws the mound of crinkled up tissues away, reaching down to pick up the one Bethany missed.

She sits back down and pulls one leg up on the bed to face Bethany. Leaning up against the pillows, Gwen motions for her to continue. By now, Bethany has calmed herself enough to tell the rest of the story.

"After he said that, I asked him what we have done. He goes off on a tangent about mom, and how she lied to him, how he is glad he found out the truth, and there is no reason to think of him and his well being."

"Wow, he is a piece of work."

"I know. I tried to plead with him and tell him we have considered his feelings after mom died, but it didn't matter." Bethany uses another tissue to wipe away the final tears.

"Well, screw him then." Gwen jumps up and makes her way to the door. "You know what this calls for?"

"What?"

"Ice cream, let's go." She takes Bethany's hand.

Not realizing I was listening, I run for the couch as soon as I hear them opening the door. I know I should not be spying on them, but I can't help it. I need to know what happened with the phone call.

As I stand to grab the journal off the end table. I stop and watch them enter the living room when Gwen gives me a 'not now' look.

"We will be back, Luthor."

"Where ya goin?"

"It's Narnia business." Bethany giggles.

Both girls grab their shoes and their jackets and head out the door, leaving me behind. Shrugging it off, I grab the journal and sit down to do some writing.

January 10th

I don't understand what is happening. Bethany called Joe, and something transpired between them, but I don't know what. She hasn't told me, but I have a feeling Gwen knows. They both left without me after doing some serious talking in Gwen's room. So alas, here I sit, journal in hand. I don't have a lot of thoughts right now, but I feel the need to write what I do know.

I can't get my mind off of Camelot. I only saw the area for a brief minute, but something about it feels different. I can't put my finger on what, but it's something. Thinking back, I remember the few people walking the streets. Do they call them streets? It was all dirt, so who knows. Note to self, find out what they call it.

A few vendors lined the area selling their wares. The canopies hung from the buildings they stood in front of, and you could hear them shouting to the people walking by. Women carried baskets with food, others having things like flowers or fabric. None of them looked like they had much money with their dirty faces, and their torn clothing. The scarves on their heads looked ragged, and the smell was nauseating.

That's all I can remember; a few vendors, a few people, and a small view of what I am sure is a much larger town. I told myself I will not worry about it until after school, and I won't. Mr. Testerman seems like an understanding man, but who am I kidding?

Well, gotta go. Someone is knocking at the door.

I get up and place the journal on the end table. As I walk towards the door, the person on the other side knocks again. "Coming."

Opening the door, I find a gentleman in a messenger uniform, almost like UPS but not with the tight shorts they wear. "Mr. McAlester?"

"Yes."

"I have a letter for you. Can you please sign here?"

I take the clipboard from him and sign my name on the dotted line. He hands me the letter, I thank him, and close the door.

I flip it through my fingers and realize there is no return address on it. As I look at my name on the front of the envelope, I recognize the handwriting immediately. *This is impossible.* This is not something that can happen, right? I stare at it for a minute longer, trying to wrap my mind around it. How is my mother sending me a letter?

My train of thought is broken when the front door slams into my back. I hurl forward onto my hands and knees. I hear a gasp behind me as a set of hands grab my shoulders. "Are you ok?"

"I am fine." I grunt as I get to my feet, picking the letter up off the floor on my way up.

"Sorry." She wipes some dust off my shirt.

"It's fine." I walk away.

"I need to speak with you, may we sit?"

"Sure, let me get some ice first."

Angelic takes her place in one of the armchairs and I take my usual spot at the edge of the couch. I wait patiently for her to speak, but she only stares at the floor.

"What is it?"

"It's Gwen."

"What about her?"

Angelic takes a deep breath through her nose before explaining. "I am worried for her. I understand she has been through a lot and there is a lot she can handle. However, these trials she will have to go through will test her beyond limits she would not think possible."

"Can you tell me about them?"

"Unfortunately, no. Only the guardians themselves know what they will be, but only when they show themselves."

"When who shows themselves?"

"Not who, but what."

"Who, what, huh?"

"The trials are challenges. The challenges present themselves when the time is right. The guardian will not know what the challenge is until it's ready to begin."

"I see. So, do you need something from me?"

"I need you to monitor her. Let me know if you see any changes in her behavior like mood swings, outbursts of anger, that sort of thing."

"No offense, but she is a woman, isn't that normal anyway?"

"I don't find this humorous in any form."

I don't respond as she makes her way to the door. She grabs the handle and turns it slightly. What she says next cuts into me. "You, Mr. McAlester, will be her downfall. It's up to you to change the outcome." She walks out the door.

What does she mean? Was the comment I made about women hurtful enough to say that in return? Does she not realize it was all in good fun? She left me here stunned and confused. While in thought, the door opens again.

"Angelic?" Gwen takes a spoon of ice cream from her cup.

"Yeah."

"You ok?" Bethany repeats Gwen's movement with her own ice cream.

"Yeah. Nothing for me? Fine, be that way."

"Oh, stop." Gwen throws a bag at me.

I open it and find my own cup of ice cream. Crinkling the bag, I throw it back at her, but miss.

"I hope your aim with a sword is better than your throwing arm." Bethany's insult is nothing compared to Angelic's.

I lower my head and say my thanks before going to my room. I can hear them talking behind me, but I let it be and close my bedroom door behind me, listening as I lean against it.

"What was that all about?"

"No idea. I was waiting for an insult back, but nothing. Something happened while we were gone."

"I know, Bethany, but the question is, should I ask him about it or leave it be and let him come to me?"

"I say let him come to you. You know how he can get snippy even if you are trying to help."

"True. So, do you feel better?" Gwen puts an arm around Bethany's shoulders and walks down the hallway.

"Yeah. I still don't know what to think about it though."

"Leave it. If this is how he wants to be, then it's what it is. Nothing you can do will change it."

"I hope you're right." Bethany breaks from Gwen's grasp and goes to her room, leaving Gwen standing alone.

"Ok then, guess I'll go to my room too."

As she makes her way a few feet, she realizes she left her phone on the end table. Turning back around, she's stopped by a figure in white blocking her way. It's tall and she can't tell if it's male or female. There is a glow around it, causing her to squint.

"Who are you?"

"I am here to bring you your first challenge."

The figure's voice is high-pitched, but very sinister. The hairs on Gwen's arms stand as it speaks.

"So be it."

"Only time can heal all wounds. Take some time, for there's an adventure soon. Some may die and some may live, but be careful if it's your heart you give. With each breath your journey lengthens and step by step your wits will strengthen."

Before Gwen responds or it says anything else, the light blinds her completely and the figure is gone. She looks down to find a small piece of parchment in the middle of a slightly scorched piece of carpet. "Well, there goes the deposit."

Once in my room, I lay the envelope on the bed. Beginning to get dressed in something a little more fitting for bed, I turn the music on low and crawl under the covers. I slowly loosen the flap on the envelope to see what's inside, and it's a hand-written letter. I pull it out and behind it's an eight by ten picture of her and my father. I leave it in there for now and sit back to read what it says.

Luthor,

My sweet boy. Don't be mad at her, but I asked Angelic to mail this to you before I left for France. I told her if anything should happen to me, I wanted to make sure this got to you and not lost somewhere. Luthor, this picture is the first thing your father, and I had together. Treasure it. Show it to your sister when you think she is ready. I love you sweet boy.

I take the letter and the picture and hold it to my chest as I sink down in my bed. This is how I want to sleep tonight.

Nosey much?

I wake to find Gwen sleeping on the couch, still in the same clothes she was wearing last night, her hair a disheveled mess. I bend over and pull the throw blanket a little higher over her shoulders. She squirms but doesn't wake up. As she moves her arm, a piece of paper falls out of her hand. Grabbing it, I unroll it and read what it says. *'Only time can heal all wounds. Take some time for there's an adventure soon. Some may die, and some may live, but be careful if it's your heart you give. With each breath your journey lengthens and step by step your wits will strengthen.'*

"This must be the first challenge."

"Luthor, what are you doing?"

Her eyes widen when she sees what I am holding. I place it on the coffee table and sit on the couch next to her. "Where do you get it?"

"Not where, but when. When the both of you went to your rooms, I came back out here and there it was."

"The paper?"

"No, a person. It was super bright and didn't say anything other than they were here to bring me the first trial. Then they read the parchment and poof, gone." Gwen looks over at the carpet and then to me.

"So that's where that came from. I wondered why it crunched when I stepped on it."

"Yeah, I'll have to speak with Angelic about it."

"It's not your fault. I am sure they can fix it."

I reach for her and guide her body to position her head on my lap. I stroke her hair and wait for the right moment to ask her the important question.

"I already know what you are thinking, Luthor."

"Do you now?"

"You want to know what I am going to do."

"You are correct."

"Well, I have no idea." She grabs the paper off the coffee table and opens it again.

As she reads it to herself, I can feel her body tense up next to me.

"You know you got this right?"

"Alone, I have to do this alone."

"It doesn't mean we won't be there to support you."

"I know."

"Hey love birds, what's for breakfast?" Bethany makes her way to the kitchen.

"I am laughing on the inside imp-fish."

"Oh, ouch." She pokes her head around the wall and places her hand on her chest. "I am dying, that insult is so good."

"You two are ridiculous." Gwen rises to her feet.

She begins to fold the blanket, and as she gets to the second fold, she begins to slow down. I stare at her, waiting for her to say something, but she doesn't. She stands there, staring off into space, her mouth slightly open. It lasts a few seconds, and then she snaps out of it and finishes folding.

"Ya good?"

"Huh? Oh, yeah, I am good."

"So, waffles, eggs, cereal, or a baby's soul?"

"You really are a twisted individual." I throw a pillow at her.

"Are you cereal? Get it? Cereal? It's a breakfast joke." She throws the pillow back.

"And a bad one." Gwen places the pillow on the couch.

We sit around the table and each of us chose something different to eat. I decide blueberry Eggos are what I was craving. Pop those bad boys into the toaster and in two minutes I have crunchy goodness smothered in butter and syrup. Gwen goes for her usual bowl of Apple Jacks, and Bethany goes for her strawberry Toaster Strudels.

There isn't much talking, and I can tell Gwen is deep in thought about the trial note she received. She is right, she must do this on her own, but I wish I could help her like she helped me. The hardest part is it being so vague and none of us even know what the trial really is. Gotta love solving riddles. You'd swear Bennu wrote it.

"So, what are we doing today?" Bethany's words break my train of thought.

"What?"

"What. Are. We. Doing. Today?"

"I am not old or deaf, just not paying attention, and I don't know."

"I figure Angelic will be down soon to give us our daily tasks."

"Ok, I get she is watching over us, but since when is she in charge of us?" Bethany has her mouth full. A bit of frosting sits on the side of her lip and I can't help but laugh at her. "What?"

"Saving it for later?" I point to her face.

She wipes all parts of her face until she gets to it. "It's the best part after all."

"You are right though, after all, she is your guardian, not ours."

"That's not what I."

"I'll go speak with her about it now."

Gwen cuts off Bethany, not even looking in our direction. She places her napkin in her bowl and heads for the door. Bethany looks at me with questioning eyes. I shrug and go back to my waffles.

"So, you are going to just sit there?"

"What am I supposed to do?"

"Go after her."

"Listen, we already talked this morning."

"And?"

"And, she got her first trial."

"Are you serious? Why am I now finding out? What is she going to do? What is it? Does she know when it will happen? Is there something we can do for her? What does it say? Tell me you are going to do something; you are going to do something, right?"

"Are you finished?"

"Yes, I am just."

"I know, so am I. You know she is not going to tell us anything if she doesn't want to. In addition, this is something she has to figure out on her own. They are her trials and there is not much for us to do. If we try to intervene when we shouldn't, it could make things harder for her. Got it?"

"Got it."

"Good. Now, we shall clean up and go after her."

"You are impossible."

"Tell me something I don't know."

Gwen makes her way up to see Angelic. Without even knocking, she walks in the door and through to the kitchen, finding Angelic sitting at the table reading a book and eating her own breakfast.

"What is this?"

"We need to talk."

"I see." Angelic remains calm, turning to face Gwen. "What is it we need to discuss?"

"I think there should be some type of clarification on what it's we are all doing here."

"Please, go on."

"Well, what exactly is your role other than to be Bethany's guardian?"

"Well, for starters," Angelic begins to stand, "I am only the temporary guardian. Bethany came into her own sooner than she should have, so in this case, there is no one ready for her yet. Secondly, I am here to look out for the three of you. I have been positioned here as a guardian for all of you until the council sees fit and you will be capable of handling things on your own. Lastly, I am here to guide you through everything coming in the future. Does that explain it?"

"Not quite. So, you are telling me, we are not on our own, and we have to have a babysitter to tell us what we can and can't do, and when to do it?"

"If you put it that way, yes." Angelic leans back, resting her rear on the edge of the table.

"What if we don't want it?"

"You don't have a choice."

"We always have a choice."

"Not this time." Angelic stands again and makes her way slowly down the hall. "Come with me."

It takes a minute to find her footing before Gwen can follow as Angelic guides her to the den. The room is dimly lit, and the curtains are closed as she pulls a book from the shelf while Gwen enters the room. She takes a seat in one of the armchairs and motions for Gwen to follow.

Being reluctant, she does it anyway, without question and without hesitation. By now, she is calmer than when he entered the apartment originally. "What is this?"

"This is a book of guidelines. Like the others, this is passed on from guardian to guardian. The council decides on a new guideline every time something comes up needing to be addressed. For example," she opens the book to the middle and begins to read aloud, "at no time shall a guardian or traveler under the age of twenty-one be permitted to act alone without the supervision of a parent or blood guardian. If neither is provided, a High Guardian will take the place and be their watcher."

"So this is what you are, a watcher?"

"Correct." She closes the book. "My job as a High Guardian is to watch over the probationary guardians or as we like to call them Neophyte Guardians. That's what you are."

"So how and when do I become a High Guardian?"

"Not for quite some time. I have been a guardian for twenty years and have only been a High Guardian for five."

"How long are you a Neophyte?"

"Until you finish your trials."

"When is that?"

"It's different for everyone."

"What comes after Neophyte?" Gwen reaches for the book.

"The next step is an Avant-Garde."

"And then?"

"Adept Guardian."

"What is the difference?" Gwen continues to skim the book, finding more and more guidelines. Some make sense and some feel senseless.

"A Neophyte is a novice. It's someone who is still learning; someone who hasn't gone through the trials."

"Me."

"Correct. An Avant-Garde is someone who has finished their trials and has come out victorious. An Avant-Garde is also one who has not fully developed their powers."

"What about the last one?"

"Adept."

"Yeah, Adept."

"An Adept Guardian is one who has finished the trials and mastered their power."

"How long does it usually take?"

"It varies really. No two guardians are the same." Angelic begins as Gwen makes her way back to the bookcase. "For some it may be 5 years between each one; others may be more or less. It really depends on the guardian and how focused and determined they are; here." She hands Gwen another book.

"Why does my Grams have all these? Wouldn't they be something the High Guardians should have stored in some musty old castle or something?"

"Your Grams was a unique woman. She lived simply and as normal as she could. What a lot of people, other than the High Guardians, don't know is that she was a High Guardian herself."

"What? Why did she never tell me?" Gwen sits back in the chair, a dumbfounded look on her face. "After all these years, how could I not have known?"

"She wanted to live as normal as she could as she gained in age. She remained a High Guardian until her death. Each High Guardian has a task assigned to them, and your Grams was a keeper."

"A what?"

"A keeper."

"What is a keeper?"

"A keeper is a High Guardian tasked with keeping the knowledge of the guardians protected and current. She was given this task because even though she was older, your Grams had a lot of fight left in her, and a vast amount of loyalty and knowledge."

Gwen lifts her chin and lets her eyes span the length of the room. There are so many things she never really paid attention to before. She was never allowed in the room as a child, so it was not until her and Luthor went on their first assignment, she had ever really been in here.

She stands and takes slow, pacing steps. Running her fingers across the books, Gwen takes the time to look closely at them. She reads the titles, feels the leather, takes them off the shelf, and flips the pages.

Angelic watches, not wanting to interrupt. In the meantime, Gwen moves from one side of the room to the other to look, touch, and embrace the history. Her mind drifts as she comes across some of the items laid out on the table and shelves. Some look old and rusted; most are made of bronze or silver. Other items have hints of marble and glass. One particular relic catches her eye. It sits on one of the bookshelves and she knows it instantly. There is something about the piece drawing her closer to it.

Reaching for the dagger, she runs her fingers over the sheath, admiring the intricate engraving created from the swirly patterns along its front. The tip is covered in silver, matching the design on its hilt. The metal is cold to the touch, and the edge is only slightly worn. The smooth feel of the marble stimulates her fingertips. Grabbing the hilt, she begins to slowly pull the dagger from the sheath. The sound of metal grinding is subtle but audible. Before she pulls it completely out, Gwen feels a strange pull come across her body.

Her eyes blur and her head begins to spin. The more she loses focus, the harder it is to keep her balance. In a daze, she can hear the sheath hit the floor, and feel the hilt in her hand.

As she drops, a set of hands catch her, lowering her to the floor slowly, but the feeling is gone as quick as it comes. Gwen lays there briefly with her eyes closed, taking in the surrounding sounds. Birds are chirping, while the sounds of people grow louder. Opening her eyes slowly, she sits up to find herself in a whole new reality. The dagger is still in her hand as she feels the ground beneath her fingertips; dirt. She looks down and finds herself in a small mud puddle, her pants filthy, and her shoes are covered.

"There you are, silly."

Gwen looks up to find a young girl dressed in purple, and the collar is embroidered with colorful leaves. The girl's long brown hair curls around her shoulders; her blue eyes catch the sun. Reaching out her hand, the girl grabs Gwen to help her up. Dumfounded, Gwen doesn't speak. The girl brushes some of the dirt off her shirt before speaking again. "What are you wearing?"

"What?"

"Your attire. Why are you wearing it?"

"This is what I always wear."

"I don't recall this type of fashion in Camelot."

Gwen pauses, the word catching her attention. "Did you say Camelot?"

"Sister, what is wrong with you? Are you ill? Should I call the physician?"

"What?" Gwen looks around. "No. What?"

"Come, we will get you bathed and changed into normal clothes. Father will be happy to know you are well. We felt we had lost you."

The girl guides Gwen through the streets, reeling from the thought of it all. The concept of being here has not fully sunk in yet, and once they arrive, she finds herself standing in front of a cabin doorway. With a creak, the young girl pushes the door open to call for her father, "Father? Father, are you home?"

"He must not be here."

"He may be at the market. Let's get you to your room so we can get you cleaned up."

"Who, who are you?"

"Seriously now."

"I am. I don't know you." Gwen begins to step back from the girl's side.

"I am your sister."

"I don't have a sister." Gwen begins to get angry.

"Why are you saying these things?" The girl begins to cry. "I am fetching the physician."

The young girl leaves, closing and locking the door behind her, trapping Gwen inside. She runs to the window and tries to pry it open, but it's stuck. Catching her fingers on the frame, a splinter of wood embeds itself. With a small screech, she repels back, moving to a small armchair beneath the light. She hadn't even realized it's night out, and the room is dark. Sitting as close to the hot fire as she can handle, Gwen leans in to find the splinter. Squeezing her finger until it's purple, she catches the tip with her nail. Grabbing at the piece of wood, she pulls it enough to release it from her finger. Following the piece of wood is a small drop of blood. Gwen wipes it on her already dirty pants and begins to take in the new surroundings. "Why am I here?" She begins to stutter from the cold air.

Realizing her pants are still wet, she sits on the floor closer to the fire. The chill begins to slowly fade away and her mind with it. It's not long before she finds herself drifting off, her eyelids turn heavy and dry.

Someone calling her name startles Gwen awake. At first, the sound is muffled and unclear, but as she wakes, she is able to understand what the girl is saying, "Guinevere, Guinevere, wake up, sleepy."

"What did you call me?" Gwen wipes her eyes, and forces herself to sit up.

"Your name."

"My name is Gwendolyn."

"Did you hit your head?"

"Lady Guinevak," the physician interrupts, "we should get her to a bed so I can examine her."

"Guinevak?"

"Yes." Guinevak turns to face Gwen.

"Nothing."

Guinevak and the physician lift Gwen to her feet and guide her to a room with a large bed. The sheets are a light pink satin, and the curtains on the four-post bed match perfectly. The room is not large by stature, but the furniture and adornments are enough to make it grander in scale. The bedposts are carved with baby cherubs, their arms raised, holding up the columns. Every piece of furniture in the room is made from dark cherry wood, and glimmers in the candlelight. The tops on the tables hugging the bed are marble and smooth. Whoever the maid is sure knows how to clean.

As Gwen makes her way to the bed, she notices something odd. The sheath from the dagger she held is sitting on the table. No dagger resides in it, but it for sure is the same one. The marble even matches the table it sits on.

"Have a seat my child. Let's get you comfortable."

"There is nothing wrong with me."

Gwen lays on her back, her head resting on the soft feather pillow, her hair sliding slightly on the soft satin covers.

"Guinevere, dear, tell me what happened. Where did you go? Why did you run off?"

"I don't know what you are talking about." She controls her breathing as the physician checks the heart and lungs.

"Father was speaking to you about an important matter, and you left." Guinevak's voice begins to crack from the tears she is holding back.

"I don't know."

Gwen feels a small prick to her arm and quickly reels back, moving to the other side of the bed. She can still see the needle in the physician's hand, and he is staring at her with compassionate eyes. "Come now, this will help you get some rest."

"I don't need help to rest, I need answers."

"As do we, but for now, rest. I will leave this here for you." He turns to Guinevak. "If she begins to get restless, you can use it later."

"Thank you." She takes the needle.

"I will take my leave now. If you need me, I will be available to you. I see no issues with her physical state. Mental, however, may be another question."

The physician makes his way to the door, turns, nods and leaves as Guinevak moves to the bedside. Gwen is still crouched in the corner, using a pillow for protection. Guinevak sits on the edge, doing her best to convince Gwen to rest.

"Come, sister," she reaches out her hand, "rest with me."

"I am not your sister. I have no sister."

"Why do you wish to hurt me so?" She rises to her feet. "So be it."

Guinevak follows the physician and makes her way to the door. As she gets closer, Gwen finally begins to move to the other side of the bed and watches Guinevak as she begins to leave.

"You know, if this is about Arthur, you shouldn't worry. He is a good man. He will make a fine king, and you will make a fine queen."

"I'm sorry, what?"

Guinevak leaves the room, locking the door behind her.

"Why am I here?!"

Story time...

Gwen wakes up later and finds herself in her own bed and it doesn't take long for her to recover from her experience in Camelot. Once out of bed, everyone sits around the living room with Angelic as Gwen tells them about what happened.

"It was scary at first, but in the end, it was interestingly thrilling. When I first woke up and found myself lying on the ground in Camelot, I was confused until I came across Guinevak."

There is a pause in Gwen's story. Bethany is sitting, facing Gwen on the couch with her legs crossed. Lowering her legs to the floor, Bethany shifts herself closer and wraps her arms around Gwen, leaning her head on her shoulder.

"I am fine. Where was I? Oh right, Guinevak."

"Interesting name." Bethany interrupts.

"Not for back then. Names may be weird to us now, but they were normal for the time-frame. Anyway, Guinevak and I met when I sat there covered in mud. I don't think she understood what I was wearing, since I was still in my normal clothes. She helped me up and took me to her home. It was a lot more sophisticated than I expected when I saw the outside, with tall pillars, white walls, marble furniture, and multiple fireplaces, but it had cabin vibes.

Once we got inside and got situated, she began to tell me I was her sister and when I told her I didn't have one, she didn't believe me. At one point, she locked me in the house. I tried my best to get out through a window, but they were sealed tight. Of course, nothing is easy, and I got a splinter and with it getting darker out, I had to use the light of the fireplace to see. I got it out, finally, and by then, Guinevak still was not back. Wet and freezing, I sat down closer to the fire and I must have fallen asleep. Next thing I know, she was waking me up, and calling me Guinevere. I tried correcting her, but she was stubborn and insisted it was my name."

"Stubborn? Sisters? Yeah, sounds about right."

"Anyway," Gwen gives me a look before continuing, "she finally came back with a physician to check me out. As persistent as I am, they were worse. They took me to a bedroom and put me to bed. Before I laid down, I noticed the oddest thing." She pauses and looks down at the dagger in her hands. Lifting it up to show us, she continues. "This was there, on one of the end tables."

"Are you sure it was this exact one?"

"Absolutely, Angelic. I finally laid back, and then Guinevak started on all her questions. Where did I go? Why did I run away? She then told me I ran off when my father was talking to me about something important. That's when he pricked me with a needle."

"Who?"

"The physician. When I would not let him give me something to help me sleep, he finally left, and I was left with her. Insistent as she was, Guinevak did her best to convince me I was her sister. What she said to me before she walked out of the room is still a question left unanswered."

"What did she say?"

"You know, if this is about Arthur, you shouldn't worry. He is a good man; he will make a fine king; and you will make a fine queen. I woke up the next day and I was in something completely different than what I fell asleep in. There was breakfast waiting for me on a tray, and someone had poured a hot bath. Before I could attempt anything, I locked myself in the room, hoping to be undisturbed, but I was not so lucky. Not fifteen or so minutes after I crawled into the bathtub, Guinevak came knocking, insisting I let her in."

"Did you?"

"Yes. I knew if I didn't she would continue to knock and call out to me until I did. That's when I realized my clothes were gone, and I would have to wear something there. Guinevak helped me lace up the long red dress, and it hit me."

Bethany, Angelic and I wait for her to go on. I can see the excitement in Bethany's eyes, and I can see the proud moment Angelic catches on what I am about to say.

"Once I looked down at the dress, I knew why I was there. I allowed Guinevak to do my hair while we talked about a few things. When I was finished, we left the room to meet someone waiting for us in the den. Then he entered the picture."

"Who? Who was it?" Bethany lifts off the couch slightly.

"Merlin." Gwen whispers with excitement.

"No." Bethany stretches it out in wonder.

"Yes."

"What did he want?" Bethany grew even more anxious.

"Me; he said he was there to help me."

"And?" Bethany coaxes me on.

"And that's when things started to get interesting. Something began to take over Guinevak, putting her in a trance. When our father came home, he found her and I on the floor with her head in my lap. He went into the den to confront Merlin, and all hell broke loose. I could hear things flying and hitting the walls, voices screaming, then suddenly, nothing." Bethany gasps. "A few seconds later, Merlin comes out, glossy eyed and scary. Once he was out the door, I made my way back into the den and found the man, our father, lying under a pile of broken wood with splinters stuck in his chest and stomach."

"Oh god." Bethany covers her face.

"Was he alive?" Angelic places a hand ever so slightly onto Bethany's arm.

"Not for long. I did my best to help him, but at one point, he knew there was nothing I could do. I sat there with him until he was gone." Gwen begins to tear up.

"Where was Guinevak?"

"She was still passed out. I had put her on the couch by then. The man's last words to me were *'marry him'*. I didn't know who *'him'* was until later, but before I go any farther, there is more to the story. While I was closing the man's eyes, Guinevak came in and saw him. As expected, she didn't take it well. I went to her and held her as long as she needed me to. Once we were good enough to go on, we knew there was planning to be done. I then realized both Guinevak and the man I called father for only a few moments were in fact family."

"You can't be serious?"

"Serious as a heart attack, Lu. I can't make this stuff up. I found a painting on the wall of the four of us. It was proof enough for me. So planning began, and we had to make our way back into the den. I noticed immediately there was something wrong with Guinevak. She reverted to the trance-like state she was in earlier in the day. I couldn't figure out what was causing it until I was close to the fireplace and felt dizzy and lightheaded. When I turned away, it subsided. When I turned back towards the fire, I started feeling sick again. I knew it was something in the fire, so I doused it with pitchers of water from all the rooms, and as soon as I did, Guinevak was fine. I sent her to the living room while I searched for papers giving us any sign of what to do next. I didn't quite find a will, but I did find some type of lease agreement between our father and the king. Simply put, we were screwed. Since he had no sons, the house goes back to the king and we become servants of the court. As I finished reading it, I noticed someone else had joined the party and Guinevak took it upon herself to deal with it."

"What did she do?" Bethany giggles, taking a sip of her soda.

"Hit him over the head with a piece of broken wood and knock him out." We all laugh for a moment. "When I realized it was Merlin, my heart dropped, but I couldn't tell Guinevak. When he came to, we explained why she hit him, and he denied everything. When I explained the bit about the fire, he did some investigating of his own and noticed something was off about the ashes. He took some with him and left."

"You let him go after what he did to your father?"

"I believed him when he said it was not him, Lu. There is a part I left out from when I first met him. At one point, while his back was turned away from me, I could hear him chanting something. It was at that moment Guinevak first went into her trance."

"It's important information to leave out."

"I know, Angelic. There was so much happening, it's hard to remember every detail, but I digress. By the way, never call him Wizard Boy, he doesn't like it. Once Merlin was gone, Guinevak told me her plan and servants from the castle came and cleaned up the den, without lighting the fireplace. We both decided to get some rest. As soon as I fell asleep, I woke up here."

"Wow, some story."

"Yup. Maybe next time you can come with me, Bethany."

"That would be amazing."

"So, what was Guinevak's plan?"

"Gwen?" Angelic prompts Gwen to answer.

She has her back to Angelic and only turns her head to answer. "I am supposed to marry Arthur, and she will be one of my ladies-in-waiting until she marries one of the Knights of the Round Table."

She walks to the kitchen and leaves the three of us wondering.

I retreat to my room to contemplate the story Gwen told us. Marry Arthur? Are they serious? I honestly don't want to think about the fact I could lose my best friend to a king. I shake the thought from my mind for now and concentrate on the fact the end of my high school career is only days away, and I still have to take the final test for my second correspondence course.

I swing my legs around on my bed and land on my stomach. Leaning forward over the edge, I pull up the blanket to find the "textbook", I use the term loosely because it's more like a small packet they sent.

I have already read the majority, but there are a few pages I need to go over again. I give the test an overview before setting it aside and working my way back through the pages. Some of it's pretty common sense, but other things are a little more interesting. The book covers things like CSI work, being a Corrections officer, joining a police department, etc. In the back of the book, it gives a list of all the jobs I can do if I want to pursue a criminal justice degree.

As I stop to read them, a light knock lands on the door. Before I can answer, Gwen walks in and makes herself comfortable next to me on the bed.

"Whatcha readin?"

"Homework."

Gwen laughs at me, knowing I hate doing this, but I have no choice.

"It's really not funny, ya know?"

"I know." she continues to giggle, "but your sad panda face is so stinking cute." She grabs my chin and shakes my head as she says it.

"Seriously?"

"Poor sport." Gwen snatches the book from my hands. "So, what do we have here? Oh, a list of jobs? Planning on switching careers, are we?" She slides from the bed and begins pacing as she reads the job descriptions aloud.

"Let's see, we have a Probation Officer." She pauses, "Oh, they can make almost forty-two thousand a year." She looks over to me. "Nice."

I hop off the bed and go towards her, "Can I have it back, please. I have to take this test."

As I reach for the book, she turns away from me and continues, "Forensic Science Technician, oh, fifty-five thousand, Police Officer, Correctional Officer, Private Detective, Oooh! You can own your own detective agency. I can see it now, you are sitting behind your desk in a smoky and dim lit room. A fedora and trench coat sitting on the coat rack in the corner and a bottle of whiskey hides in the bottom desk drawer. You look up as the door opens, and a damsel comes in, legs for days with her red lipstick and a wide-brimmed hat covering half her face in shadows."

"You aren't funny." I try to take the book again.

She places it behind her back with one hand and puts the other hand on my arm. "Oh mister, can you help me?" She begins, doing her best Marilyn Monroe impression. "I think someone kidnapped my husband and I have to find him." She bats her eyes.

I take my free arm and wrap it around her waist. If she wants to play the game, we are playing by my rules. Once my arm is around her, I pull her in with force. She lets out a little yelp of surprise, but before she can say anything, I lay a kiss on her lips. She backs away, and I can tell by the shocked look in her eyes she was not playing any more.

"Why?" She begins to back away slowly.

"It was in fun, ya know, playing along."

"It's not funny."

She turns away, but before she can make it out the door, I grab her arm and turn her towards me, "I am sorry."

She doesn't reply, and I can tell she wants to forgive me, and she doesn't want to be mad at me for it. Her eyes turn red, a tear or two start to fill the inner corners as she takes a deep breath and lets it out. Gwen breaks free of my hold and leaves the room.

I know there is no point in trying to go after her. She is like me, when she is upset she has to deal with it on her own. So, I let her walk out, leaving me standing there in my own pit of stupidity, knowing I'm the reason she feels like this.

Who was that?

Sunday rolls around like any other day. We sit around the table, eating our breakfast, waiting to see what Angelic has in store for us. No one speaks, and as the expression goes, you could cut the tension with a knife. I can't handle the quiet, so I decide to leave the girls sitting there. As I get up, I can see Gwen out of the corner of my eye, watching me leave the room. I hear slight whispers as I get farther away, but I don't bother trying to listen.

I venture back to my room and crawl into my favorite spot, my bed. Since I really didn't do much reading after she left the room last night, I know I have to finish the criminal justice book by tonight. With school tomorrow, I want to make sure I have this out of the way.

I pull the test from the back of the book and lay on my stomach. Starting from the beginning, I go from question to question. When I make it through all twenty-five questions, I look up at the clock, realizing it has taken me almost two hours. I am terrible at tests, it's a lot harder than I thought.

Taking one last look, I fold the paper and put it in the envelope. I carry it with me to the kitchen to get a stamp out of the drawer. The apartment is quiet, and I can't hear anything from Gwen or Bethany's bedroom. Did they leave and not tell me? Where did they go? I am happy the two of them are growing closer, but this means I am growing farther from them.

I grab the stamp and put it on the envelope. I know the mail is not coming today, but if I don't put it in the mailbox now, I will forget it in the morning. I open the front door to come face to face with Guiney, Bethany's best friend. She has her fist up, ready to knock, but lowers it slowly and stands there. "Guiney."

"Luthor." She almost sounds disgusted saying my name. I never know how to tell if it's me, or her personality. "Is Bethany here? She is not answering her cell."

"I have no idea where she is. You can check her room."

Guiney pushes past me and walks toward Bethany's room. I go out the door to put the test in the mailbox. Out of the corner of my eye, I can see someone lurking in the hallway. I stop briefly and turn, but they are gone.

"She is not here." Guiney leans in the doorway.

"Yeah, I know." I stand at the entrance, staring at the empty hallway.

Guiney steps closer and waves her hand in front of my face. "Earth to Luthor."

"If I see her I'll tell her to call you."

"Yup." And she is gone.

As soon as I hear the outer door of the apartment building close, a relaxed feeling comes over me and I am able to focus. Who was that in the shadows? Where did they go?

I go back into the apartment and decide what I need now is a snack and a little music to clear my head. Going to the kitchen, I rummage through the cabinets, looking for something to satisfy this need for, whatever it's.

As I go door to door, and shelf to shelf, I get more and more anxious. It's not really about the food, it's a gut feeling inside you that something isn't right. My mind immediately goes back to the hallway and the person lurking in the shadows. I sit back against the table and do my best to focus on the image of the person, straining to pick out some detail. The harder I try, the less I can come up with.

I go to my room and grab a flashlight from under my bed, debating in my head whether to grab the sword. Changing my mind, I go to Gwen's room and grab her dagger instead. Something more lightweight will be easier to handle if there really is someone hiding, waiting to get me by surprise.

Mission Impossible style, I creep out my front door and close it slowly, doing my best not to make any noise. I check both sides of the hallway before I close it completely and continue to my right. The hallway is lit, but it's not very bright. It stretches a hundred feet or more, and the farther it goes, the darker it gets. I wait to use the flashlight until I actually have to, and the first door I come to is apartment one. There is a nice old woman living there who would always give us pennies on Halloween. Not something every kid wants, but as I get older, I know it's all she can do. I jiggle the handle quietly to check if it's unlocked, nope, so I move to the next door. Apartment three houses a man who pretty much keeps to himself. You never hear any loud noises, no parties, nothing. To be honest, I don't know if I have ever really seen him outside of the apartment. I jiggle the handle again and find it locked.

The last door in the hallway leads to the basement where all the storage units are. I never really venture down there since everything we own is in our apartment. My mother never really said whether there was something down there or not. Now I am second-guessing myself, so I might as well go look. The squeal of the hinges vibrates through the hallway. "A little WD40?" I whisper to myself.

I take the first step and look on the stairway wall for a light switch. There is no light on the stairwell, so using my flashlight is my only option at this point. With each step, I can hear the creaking of the wood beneath my feet. The old wood could easily give way and I would not have any warning. With the flashlight in one hand and the other hand on the railing, I make it to the bottom step.

I find the light switch, and as I flick it to the on position, I can hear the sizzle and crackle of the lights coming on. There are large can lights hanging from wires in the ceiling. The fluorescent yellow glow casts creepy shadows on the wall. The basement runs the length of the apartment building and only houses about six rooms. Each one is numbered for all the apartments. That is until I make it to the end of the row.

I stand in front of a door with no number, no name, and no lock. As I reach for the handle, I am startled by the sound of something hitting the ground. I turn with my flashlight, but no one is there. I direct the light towards the ground, expecting to find a mouse or some other fuzzy rodent, but there isn't anything there either. A look of panic breaks across my face, triggering beads of sweat on my forehead.

I return my focus to the mystery room, so I reach for the door again as another sound makes its way to my ears. I whip around again, and like before, nothing. I don't hesitate this time and grab the handle to swing the door open. I reach for the dagger in my belt and sweep the flashlight side to side. The room looks to be empty, but something about it doesn't feel right to me.

I turn and close the mysterious door behind me. As I turn back around to find the storage room for our apartment, I am blindsided by a figure in a hooded cloak.

As it floats before me, its hand clenches my throat and its pointy nails dig into my skin. I am able to grab the front of its cloak and give the figure a shove. It holds a tight grip around my neck. Thinking quickly, I throw my weight to the left and knock us both down to the ground. As we land, I am able to break free and reach to my hip for the dagger, but it's not in my belt anymore. I remember having it in my hand and realize I must have dropped it when we both fell. I use the flashlight to search for it, but before I can get to it, the figure grabs me by my right ankle and I slam to the floor again. I use the other foot to kick at its face, but its moves are a split second faster than mine. As my leg pushes forward, its hand clenches around my ankle like a vice.

The figure turns to its side, twisting my ankle, and I cry out in pain. As I try to twist around to loosen its grip, I find my opening. I throw every bit of force I have into my left leg and slam my foot into the creature's face. It let outs a screech, and I am completely stunned. It's a woman, the person in the cloak is a woman. The woman releases my ankle and brings her hands to her face.

"You fool! You have no idea what you have done." I stand in stunned silence as she begins to growl and moan, huffing with each breath. "This is only the beginning."

She hisses, and with a flap of her arms, she disappears in a puff of black smoke, choking me till it disappears.

I bring my hand to my chest to steady my heart, but it doesn't work. "Luthor! Are you down there?"

"Yeah."

I can hear her running down the stairs and I grab her instantly. "I am so sorry."

She releases herself from my arms and sits at the bottom of the stairs. She notices my torn shirt and an instant look of fear and worry crosses her face. "What happened?"

"Long story, come on." I guide her upstairs, knowing this is something to discuss with Angelic.

I pull her by the arm as Bethany meets us in the hallway and follows closely behind. I don't even bother to knock this time. I open the door and look for Angelic.

"This must be important if you're barging in here so rudely." She scolds as she comes around from the hallway.

"It's."

"Well, then sit, if you must, and tell me what this is about."

The four of us sit around the living room and I take a breath before beginning my recollection of what happened. "I left the apartment to put a letter in the mailbox for tomorrow. I caught something out of the corner of my eye, but when I turned, it was gone. I went back into the apartment, but I couldn't shake the feeling there was something going on."

"And?" Bethany interrupts.

"And give me a minute." I glare at her, "I thought I could shrug it off, so I went to the kitchen for something to snack on, but the feeling was still gnawing at me, so I decided to investigate. I grabbed a flashlight from my room and your dagger from yours." She takes the dagger from me with a look of confusion or disappointment. "I went back to the hallway and checked the other two apartment doors, but they were locked."

"Why would you check there?"

"Ya never know, Angelic."

Angelic lifts her shoulders and tilts her head to suggest she understands. I take a moment to look out the window. The sun is setting, and my stomach is growling.

"Where was I?"

"Other apartments."

"Oh, right."

Gwen has been quieted the whole time, and I wonder what she is thinking. Normally by this point, she would have put her two cents in about the situation and we'd be coming up with some kind of solution to the problem. Is she off her game? Is there something else on her mind? I shake it off and continue. "I checked the basement next. It was quiet, and the lighting sucked, but I found one room with no number or name on it. The door was unlocked, and the room was empty. I thought I heard something down there, but I didn't see anything until I came back out of the room. I was blindsided by someone in a hooded cloak. Their face was covered, and their hands looked old and wrinkled with long sharp nails."

"Any idea who it could be?"

"No, but at first I thought it was a guy, but as we were fighting, I got a kick to its head and it screamed like a girl. When it backed off, it spoke. *'You fool!'* It said to me, *'You have no idea what you have done.'* Then she disappeared in a puff of smoke, and you called down to me."

I can see Gwen pondering in that nerdy brain of hers. "So, a hooded figure with magic powers and it's a woman? Then there is Merlin, Guinevak, my father." she put her fingers in quotes, "King Arthur, and the Knight of the Round Table. Am I missing anything?"

I shake my head and look at Angelic and Bethany. The two of them shake their heads no, so we move on. I turn to Bethany again. "Oh, Guiney stopped by."

"What did she want?"

"No idea, I told her I would have you call her."

Bethany gets up and goes into the other room. I am left with Angelic staring out the window and Gwen deep in thought. I get myself up and go to the kitchen for something to drink.

As I make my way, I can hear Bethany in the other room, and she sounds panicked. Waiting on the drink, I quietly step closer to the door of the office. It's closed, but I can hear well enough. I close my eyes and focus my attention on what she is saying.

"I know. We can talk about it tomorrow." Then a pause. "No, I haven't told Luthor yet. Alright, I'll tell him." Pause, "Okay! Bye."

As soon as I hear her say bye, quickly and quietly, I step away from the door and toward the kitchen. I hear the door to the office open and Bethany lets out an exhale of frustration. "Who was it?"

Gwen and Angelic turn their attention to Bethany from the living room. I pop my head out of the kitchen doorway. "Who was what?"

"Listening, who was listening?"

No one speaks, and she gets even more aggravated. Her face begins to turn an unhealthy shade of red, and her fingertips curled into a fist. "No one? Really? I heard you walking down the hall. I am not stupid."

"Calm down Bethany." Angelic gets up and makes her way over to her.

Bethany takes a breath and before she can speak again, I cut her off. "It was me."

"Why? What business do you have listening to my conversations?"

"I am your brother and it's my job to look out for you. When I can hear you from the kitchen, it's pretty obvious something is up." I place my hands on my hips and wait for her to reply.

The look in her eyes shows it was time to spill it. "I guess it's my turn for story time."

We go back to the living room and sit in our regular spots. Bethany rests her elbows on her legs and continues to ring her hands together. Keeping her face down, she begins her story. "It was a while ago. I was in class and I started to feel sick. I made it to the wastebasket, but Mrs. Granada sent me to the restroom anyway. Guiney went with me and I washed my face and took something for my stomach. As we stood there, I get lightheaded and almost fell, but Guiney caught me. Once Guiney got me back on my feet, we made our way to the nurse's office. Guiney left me there while she made her way back to class."

"Why didn't you tell us?" Angelic places a soft hand on Bethany's arm.

"Oh wait, there's more. She asked me the basic questions like what I had to eat and drink. Then she disappeared for a few minutes and came back with a granola and some concoction she had come up with. It tasted horrible, but she insisted I drink all of it and eat the granola, so I sipped it and ate at the bar. Within a few minutes, I began to feel better, so I hopped down from the table and made my way to her office, when a smell hit my nose. The smell was like the 'tea' she had me drink, but I didn't see the nurse anywhere, so I called out to her. She popped up behind me and scared the crap out of me. I turned to face her and noticed Mrs. Easegrom's shoulders were set back, her eyes were dilated, and she seemed a little tense. You could see the red veins weaving their way through the whites of her eyes, and she had a smell coming off her, not like the tea, but stronger, almost metallic like blood.

I convinced her I was okay and tried to leave the office. I knew something was up, so I made my way out the door, keeping my eye on her the whole time. As I watched, the expression changed almost instantly. Mrs. Easegrom's lip began to curl on one side, and her eyes became wide and bright. I shut the door behind me and ran back to class."

"This is getting to be a little more complicated than I thought." Gwen interrupts her.

"But wait, there's more. When I got home, we fought. It's one of the reasons I didn't say anything. When I got to school the next day, there was a surprise waiting for me. Gabriele was there and asked me to the Winter Ball."

"Really?" Gwen beams. "What did you say?"

"Yes, of course." The girls giggle together.

I clear my throat, hoping for her to continue with the story. "Party pooper." Gwen pouts and turns to Bethany. "What else?"

Bethany recalls the moments exactly as she remembers them. "We made our way to class, but not before running into Mrs. Easegrom. She looked disheveled and weak. Her face was pale, but her cheeks were pink. Her normal scrubs looked like she had rolled through a mud pit. The pockets were torn, and she was only wearing one shoe. We ran to her and did our best to help her. She had a slight limp, and you could tell she was in pain. I asked her what was wrong, and she said, 'A person in the office, fire, hand' and then collapsed.

We got Mrs. Reigina to come and help, then Guiney ran to get Mr. Testerman while I stayed with Mrs. Reigina. I grabbed the nurse's head as Mrs. Reigina stood and walked a few paces with my phone, so she was out of earshot. She seemed frantic and nervous, and I did my best to listen to what was being said. All I could hear was 'No. I know what this means.' There was a pause. 'Fine!'

"Then what happened?" Gwen thrives with anticipation.

"Mrs. Reigina left me again and made her way to the nurse's office. As she disappeared around the corner, Guiney came back with Mr. Testerman. He dropped to his knees to check her out. I looked up at Guiney, and the look between us was understanding with no words. We were both concerned, and both in disbelief." Bethany stops again and gets up to make her way to the kitchen. "Something to drink?" She points at the three of us. We shake our heads no, and she disappears.

"Who is Mrs. Easegrom? Is she another person?"

"That's what Guiney, and I wondered too." Bethany answers as she makes her way back to us. "While we waited, Mr. Testerman pulled something out of his pocket. When I asked him what it was, he hesitated before letting me know it was a wakening draft."

"Interesting." Angelic ponders.

"After he gave her the wakening draft, she came to, but she was still disoriented. Mr. Testerman and Mrs. Reigina helped her back to her office, and we were forced to go to class."

"Has anything else happened since?" I try to piece it all together.

"Nothing."

I start the list in my head, then out loud. "So, let's evaluate, shall we? We know Mr. Testerman is Tristan, a Knight of the Round Table. Guinevak is your sister in Camelot. She is supposed to marry a knight, and you are supposed to marry King Arthur. Your father is dead, and Merlin is supposedly to blame, although he admits his innocence. There is a hooded woman trying to end me, but we have no idea who she is. Mrs. Easegrom and Ms. Reigina may be part of the whole thing, but there is no guarantee yet. Am I missing anything?"

"I think that about covers it."

"So, the next question is, what is our next step?"

"To be honest, Bethany, I think we need to find out what connection there is between Mrs. Easegrom and Mrs. Reigina. We also need to figure out if there is anyone else out there we may be missing. Right now, everyone in our lives needs to be looked at."

"Everyone?" Bethany seems unsure.

"Everyone."

"Well, I guess we have some homework to do."

"Any other thoughts besides that, Angelic?"

"None for now."

"Ok, ready, break." I clap my hands together and raise myself from the couch.

"You are an idiot."

"But this is why you love me." I give her a cheesy smile.

"Love is such a strong word."

"Ouch! A stab in the heart."

"Awe, poor baby."

What is that smell?

January 12th

Well, isn't this something? Here I thought I could make it until graduation without having to dive into someone else's troubles. Who am I kidding?

Too much to ask? Of course it's, but hey, it was bound to happen eventually, right? Here is the way I am spinning this, I have 9 days, 9! If you don't count the weekend, I have a week; 5 days. My correspondence classes are done, even though I have no idea what the grades are yet. The last few days Gwen and I have left will be filled with finals, half days, and getting our exit interviews with the counselor. I have to make it through finals, which will be the hardest part. Gwen, of course, has no problem since she is a brainiac. I, on the other hand, have to study.

So, long story short, I will work on Camelot and the people have come to take me away ha ha… in my off time from school.

Someone is a knock, knock, knocking on my chamber door. Gotta go.

I close the journal and drop it to the floor. "Yeah?"

"It's me!"

"Come in, Angelic."

"I will feel more comfortable if you come out."

"I'll be out in a minute."

"I will meet you in the living room."

I throw on a pair of jeans and make my way to the living room. Gwen and Bethany are already there waiting for me, both in their usual spots. Bethany is sitting in her chair and Gwen is on the couch. Angelic has placed herself on the other chair, which makes the situation feel like walking into an intervention. All eyes are on me and you could cut the tension with a knife.

"Wow, is this an intervention? Do I need to go to rehab?"

"This is not a time for jokes."

I make my way to the other side of the couch, opposite Gwen.

"Have you had any luck finding out information about our friends from beyond the pond?"

"Beyond the pond?"

"I am not good at keeping the mood light."

"It's okay, we get it, and no, at least I haven't." Gwen looks at Bethany and me, and neither of us have anything to add, other than the obvious. "We haven't exactly had a lot of time to do any research with school, homework, finals, and everything else. We will need more time."

"Understood." Angelic rises up off the chair, making her way to the door. "If you need my resources, please don't hesitate."

Angelic leaves the apartment, and the three of us are dumbfounded. "Does something seem off with her?"

"Maybe. She tried to be funny. Even that itself is off." Bethany sounds both concerned and confused.

"I am sure there is something she is not telling us, which will be nothing out of the ordinary." Gwen's voice combines sarcasm, hurt, and a hint of disgust.

"What time is it anyway?"

"Six." Gwen responds without looking at her phone, or me.

"So, dinner then?"

"I am not really hungry." Bethany begins to head to her room.

"Neither am I." Gwen follows behind.

"Well, alright-y then. Dinner for one please, Jeeves."

"I am sure there are some leftovers in the fridge. Angelic didn't make anything tonight since two of us weren't eating." Gwen comes from the hallway.

"Well, I guess I can fend for myself well enough."

I pull open the fridge door and lean forward to peer inside the abyss of leftovers, condiments, and drinks. A smell floats into my nose closely resembling a sewage dump, or maybe a baby's diaper.

"Good lord, what is that?"

I lean in closer to see if I can tell which shelf it's coming from. With as much stuff as there is in here, I can't get a good idea of what is causing the offensive odor. I close the door and grab the garbage. It's already half full, so I drag it instead of picking it up. I open the fridge again and pull things out one by one.

I start with a pile of containers I know are older than a week, and another pile I know are from the last few days. Once I get all the leftovers pulled out, I rearrange the drink items on the top self, the condiments in the door, and put the good leftovers back on the middle and bottom shelves.

I shut the refrigerator door and lean up against it as I sit Indian style on the floor. One by one, I open the containers and check the status of the contents. A few are growing friends of the furry variety, and a few others are turning into a nice soupy mess. Then, there are the few so bad, I can't even bring myself to keep the containers. Those puppies are a combination of furry friends, a soupy mess, the smell of sewage on a hot summer day, and a baby's diaper. "How did we let it get this bad?"

I finally finish with the refrigerator, and food has totally lost its appeal. After going through all those containers, I am not inclined to eat anything. '*I need to study for the finals anyway.*' I think to myself.

I make my way to my room and grab my book bag off my desk chair. It's not as heavy as it has been in past years, and I am thankful. I never understood how more students don't develop back problems from the weight of all the books they have to carry.

The first two finals I need to do are history and science. Of course, those are my two hardest subjects. *"Luthor."* I go to my bedroom door and open it, but no one is there. *"Seriously, Luthor?"*

"What?"

As I turn to make my way back to my bed, I am surprised by the appearance of a figure in white. I stumble back, and the figure laughs. It's a laugh I have heard many times before, a laugh I never thought I would hear again. "Hello Luthor."

"Zeus."

"My friend." He embraces me. "How have you been?"

"Not bad." I give him a questioning look. "What are you doing here?"

"What, I can't come for a visit?"

"Uh, huh."

"Fine then, down to business." He sits on the edge of my bed. "I have heard of your mother's passing and I have come to see what I can do to be of help."

"I appreciate it, but there is nothing to be done." The reminder of my mother turns my mood from one of excitement to one of hurt.

"I can see by your change in expression that all is not well."

"You are correct." I pull my chair near him and sit down.

"And there is nothing I can do?"

"Nothing."

He pauses for a minute, and I can tell he is contemplating something. His eyes shift, and he mumbles something I can't hear. Within seconds, he takes my hand. "Do you trust me?"

He doesn't even give me a chance to answer, before we are back in the one place feeling like my second home; Olympus. I have to blink a few times to adjust my vision, but once I do I am overwhelmed with what I see.

The shacks originally housed by the minor gods are gone, the bridge is still intact, and the portal continues to shimmer in the sunlight. "Luthor!" She reaches out to me.

I don't go to her, and I can see by her vacant expression that it hurts her feelings. What does she expect? I was not chummy then, and I am not going to change . "Hera."

She clears her throat and composes herself. "How are you?"

"Fine."

"Will we always be this way?"

"After what you did?"

"I understand." She takes her place next to Zeus.

"There are a few others who would like to say hello." Zeus raises his arm and motions toward the palace.

I turn back towards the bridge and watch as three of the most influential people come towards me. As if something out of a movie, Athena, Artemis, and Apollo walk in perfect formation across the bridge. The mist from the water splashes up behind them, reflecting the shimmer of the portal.

I make my way towards them without hesitation. As I get closer, Artemis breaks formation and begins to run towards me with open arms. Once she hits me, we both topple to the ground laughing. Laying there for a minute, I look up and Athena is standing over me. "Hello Luthor."

"Athena." I reach out my arm to her. She clasps my wrist in the normal greeting and helps me to my feet.

Apollo does the same for Artemis, and the four of us stand in a circle, taking a moment to appreciate the company. "How are you?" Artemis beams.

"I am okay."

Her tone changes at my lack of enthusiasm. "I am sorry about your mother."

"We all are." Hera adds as her and Zeus make their way towards me.

"Thank you."

"Is there anything we can do?"

"I wish there was, and I appreciate the offer. However, right now, I am trying to get through my last week of school before I have to go to Camelot."

"What is this Camelot you speak of?"

"It's a place similar to this. They have kings and queens, poor and rich. They called on me about a week or so ago, but I have been doing my best to avoid it."

"Why?"

"School, Apollo; I want to get through this last week and then I am all theirs."

"Are you sure there is nothing we can do?"

"Unless you can pass my finals for me, Zeus, there really isn't." A part of me wishes I could ask them to bypass the finals with passing grades, so I can move on with my life, and have this nightmare over.

"We can." Hera chimes in.

"Do what?"

"Bypass these finals you speak of."

"Did you?"

"Yes, I did."

"You can do that?"

"There is nothing I can't do. After all, I do owe you."

"I can't ask that of you. It would not be right."

I feel a large hand rest on my shoulder.

I turn to look at Zeus. "As much as I want to stay, I really have to go."

"I understand, take my hand."

I look at the others standing before me and smile. "I will see you soon."

Apollo waves.

Artemis smiles.

Athena bows.

Hera nods her head.

Suddenly, I am back in my room. "Until we meet again, young one." Zeus begins to dissipate into the air. "Remember, anything."

I didn't realize when I returned, my door was open. Someone clears their throat, and I turn to find Bethany standing there with a shocked and disturbed look. "Was?"

"Uh huh." I make my way to my bed to open books.

"Did you go to Olympus?"

"Yup."

"What did you do there? I thought you couldn't go back?! What did Zeus want? Do they need you? Will you take me?"

"Stop!" I interrupt her. "I'll answer your questions later. Right now, I have to study."

Bethany huffs and storms out of the room. Within seconds my phone rings, I pick it up off the bed to check the caller id, and notice it's the school. I only contemplate answering it for about a minute before I set my phone back down and open the history book.

As Gwen slowly wakes, she moves her left arm and can feel something strange at her fingertips. She wiggles them around, feeling a small mound of dry leaves. As she grabs a handful and squeezes, they crumble away.

Upon the realization, she is startled completely awake. Lifting herself to a sitting position, she frantically looks around to diagnose her surroundings. "A forest; I am in a forest. Why am I in a forest?"

As she twists from side to side, the sound of the rustling leaves crunch beneath her. The sudden racket of footsteps in the distance catches her attention and she stops, listening as the steps grow closer.

Not far from view, Gwen glimpses three men walking towards her. Two are clad in armor, and the third is dressed as a simple peasant. Quickly, she rises to her feet and scrambles to hide herself behind a tree. As the men make their way closer, she can hear their conversation.

"Yes, my lord." The peasant dressed man claims, walking a few feet behind.

"I want to make sure Lady Ragnall has everything she needs for tonight. Her closest friend is coming, and she has lost her father." One of the knights explains.

"Yes, my lord."

"Make sure you speak with the cooks so there is enough food for everyone. I will not have anyone going hungry at my table."

"Yes, my lord."

"Gawain, who is this friend you speak of, and why is this dinner so important to you? It's not as if she has never been to your house before, I am sure." The second knight wonders.

"My wife is everything to me. You will learn when you have one of your own, Lancelot."

"You know better than anyone it will never happen."

"Free spirited one, yes, I know. We must get back to the castle. Arthur will be expecting a report on his sister, and you know how impatient he can be."

"He is about as patient as a hyper squirrel."

The two men continue, not even noticing me behind the tree. As they grow farther and farther apart, she slowly makes her way out of hiding. Gwen's foot snaps a branch into pieces as she circles to the left of the tree. The servant immediately turns and their eyes lock. She slowly places a finger to her lips and pleads to him with her eyes to not say anything to the oblivious knights.

With a look of unsureness and confusion, the servant turns toward the knights and continues walking. She stands in place until she is sure they are far enough away to walk normally. Following the path of the trees to stay hidden from sight, her mind stays clear, and she does her best to focus on the surrounding noises.

After roughly ten minutes of walking, she comes up on a stone wall. It easily stands twice her height, and you can tell by the haphazard arrangement of the stones, it was not done with efficiency in mind. Gwen runs her fingers across the abrasive gray rocks and catches on a sharp corner. She pulls back suddenly and finds a cut on her left index finger. She wipes her finger on her pants and continues on.

She follows the length of the wall for around one hundred feet or so until she comes to a spot covered in ivy and dry branches. The shrubbery covering the wall also blocks her from going any further. The vines and branches intertwine with each other, creating a wall of vegetation. Gwen has no weapons with her and she doesn't want to get any more cuts or scratches. She then remembers to change. She closes her eyes, takes a deep breath and begins to feel the tingle of her body transforming.

Once the tingle begins to subside, Gwen runs her hands down her sides to feel the soft, cool touch of the leather around her waist. With her right hand, she grasps the string of her bow resting across her chest. She reaches for the dagger at her side. The metal is cool to the touch, and the point of the handle grazes the tip of her finger.

The twinkle in her eye reflects the excitement building inside her. She turns in the direction she was headed and continues along the wall, using the blade to chip away at the vines blocking her way.

Once she makes it through the wall of plants, she steps forward, breaking something hard under her foot. Gwen bends down to find a broken bottle. As she looks at the remnants of the bottle, she recognizes a smell that doesn't belong. "Sulfur?" She reaches for the largest piece of the broken bottle and inspects it. The glass smells even more strongly of sulfur than she'd expect. "Why would a bottle of sulfur be out here?"

She places the piece of glass in a pouch at her side and takes a few more steps, finding herself in front of a large wooden door. The wood is worn, but it seems sturdy enough still. What may have once been a dark walnut color has faded into an ashy gray. The handle is rusty, and the original bronze color is turning into a chipped mess.

Gwen grabs the handle and uses her thumb to press down on the lever. The door doesn't budge, and the lever only sticks. "Is it stuck or is it locked?" She takes her blade and runs it along the seam of the door, under the handle. A small clink is made when the blade comes in contact with the latch, holding it closed. "Locked, or is it?"

Holding tight to the sword with one hand, she tries to lift the latch while she holds the lever with the other hand.

"Ugh, nothing." She braces the handle and lever with her hand again and uses her shoulder to slam into the door. You can hear a crack from the door where her shoulder makes contact, and she backs away slightly to look at what she has done. "Well, this is not going to do anything; now what?"

Gwen keeps trying until it's getting dark, and her ability to see is dwindling. She stands in front of the door, trying to find a way through it. As she leans against the stone wall, doing her best to think of a plan, she can hear another set of voices coming from the road. Ducking behind one of the trees, she watches as two cloaked females make their way towards the door.

Covering her mouth to hush her breathing, she waits for them to pass. As their voices grow softer, Gwen creeps from the tree and makes her way back towards the door. She places her hand on the chipping bronze quietly and slowly. Her thumb begins to finally lower the lever to unlatch the door. As the latch clicks, she opens it only enough to squeeze through, and then shuts it behind her.

She can see a small light coming from a few feet ahead. Following the length of the wall from the inside, she makes her way towards the light. As she gets closer, she sees the two cloaked women standing over a large stone altar. Creeping her way towards them, she does her best to stay out of sight and quiet.

Once within earshot, she listens intently, and whatever it's, is not English. Gwen makes her way around to see what is on the altar in front of them. Close enough to the front, she can see the two women leaning over a black bird lying helpless on the stone. One has a blade in her hand, glowing blue, while the other is grabbing pinches of powders from small bowls and throwing them on the bird.

"Adiuro hoc spiritu tuam. Concedo hac potestate tua. Cum haec et eandem animam tuam. Fugere mecum fugite mecum Vola mecum." They keep saying the words repeatedly as they throw one powder after another.

Gwen's eyes water from the smell coming off the altar. She begins to rub them, to tame the irritation. Looking up, the black bird suddenly begins to rise into the air, causing the two women to giggle and squeal with excitement. "This is it"

"What is it?" Gwen thinks to herself, not knowing her question will be answered sooner than she thinks. As the bird dangles in the air, she notices a spark fly from its wing. Then another and another until the entire bird is engulfed in flames.

When the bird is nothing but ash, the dust begins to slowly fall back to the stone. One of the women gathers it up and places it in a small wooden bowl. The other pulls another black bird from the side of the stone and places it in the center. With the dagger in hand, she swiftly removes the bird's head at the lower part of its neck. Picking up the body, she squeezes the blood of the bird into the bowl while she begins another chant.

"Sanguis lapso resurgentis erit sanguis. Sanguis lapso resurgentis erit sanguis. Sanguis lapso resurgentis erit sanguis."

Gwen's foot shifts slightly and a branch snaps. The heads of both women whip in her direction, and she cowers to the ground, remaining as quiet as possible. The two women stare for a moment, and she can see the face of one of the women under the hood. It's Mrs. Granada, but who is the other woman?

The image of the two women fade until there is nothing left. She wakes to find herself in her own bed. "Oh crap."

I wake to a knock on my door, startling me, and I drop the history book on the floor. "Yeah?" I answer with irritation. It swings open and Gwen busts into the room. She has a look of panic on her face, her hair is disheveled, her pajama pants are on backwards, and her t-shirt is barely on.

"We have a problem."

"What?"

Gwen rushes to my bed and plops down next to me. Her frantic nature has not yet subsided, and it's making me nervous. She begins to fiddle with her finger as she sits there.

"What?"

"Mrs. Granada."

"What about her?"

"I think she is one of those people, but there is a problem."

"What is the problem?"

"I don't think she is here to help."

"How do you mean?"

"I had a dream, but it felt real, kind of like one of my visions."

"Do you think this is another trial?"

"I have no idea." She looks around "What time is it?"

I pick up my phone off the dresser and check the time. "Two a.m."

"Do you think Angelic is awake?"

"I doubt it." I set my phone back down. "Why don't you try to get some sleep and we can talk to her in the morning before school."

"Can I stay here?"

"I guess."

I really don't think it's necessary or right with how I still feel about her, but I am not going to deny her either.

Um, that's a dragon!

I wake up and turn to wrap my arm around Gwen, but she is already gone, so I fling off the covers and head for the kitchen, stopping to grab my phone. Meeting Bethany in the hallway, she looks determined to pursue something. What is it with her?

"Good morning." I enter the kitchen.

Gwen is sitting at the table, and the conversation between her and Angelic seems heated. As soon as Bethany and I enter, they stop and look up at us.

"What?" I watch their concerned faces.

"Sit down please."

"Okay."

"Both of you." She gazes at Bethany. "We need to discuss the issue at hand."

"Camelot, I know."

"It's more, so please listen. Gwen's dream is an omen to what you may be facing when you get to Camelot. She explained how she saw Mrs. Granada in her dream, and she did tell me what the dream was about."

"She is right here." Gwen blurts.

"Sorry."

"As I was saying, Mrs. Granada is, as we know, another person who is here as Tristan is. What we don't know is what her intentions are and what she has planned. For now we need to go to Tristan and see what he knows."

"I am sure he will be at one of the schools today."

"As true as that is, you will not be going to school."

"What do you mean?" Gwen sounds perturbed.

"I received a call last night from the Board of Education; a Mister Thomas Baker. Although he calls himself Dr. Baker. He said he is the Superintendent of the school district and you are cleared of your finals and will graduate as scheduled."

"Explains the phone call I got last night. I shrugged it off and didn't answer. They must have called you after." I pull my phone out and look at the time they called, and then it hit me. "Son of a."

"Language."

"They did it anyway."

"What do you mean?"

"Zeus did this even though I asked him and Hera not to."

"Did what?"

"Make it so our finals are taken care of."

"Well, that explains it. It's like him to do that, I'm sure." Gwen chuckles. "Okay, so what if Mrs. Granada is a witch or wizard or whatever they called those back then? Can she be the person who was tampering with the fireplace when I was there? Oh! Can it be the woman you fought in the basement? I think after we meet with Mr., I mean Dr. Baker, we need to meet with Mr. Testerman, or Tristan, or whatever his name is. He is bound to know something about what is going on. While we are there, we should ask him about Mrs. Easegrom too. After the story Bethany told us, I have a feeling she is part of this too. I know Bethany wants to be all "Ninja Mode" with her best friend, but I don't think she should be doing things like this on her own yet."

"I agree."

"That's all you have to say, I agree?" Gwen's voice is harsh.

"I figured you had more to add first."

"Oh. There is more. I never told you about the actual dream."

"What about it?"

"Well, besides Mrs. Granada, there was another woman. I couldn't see who she was, but she was just as twisted. Before I even got to that point though, I had to hide from two knights and a squire as soon as I woke up there."

"Do you know who they are?"

"Lancelot and Gawain."

"Who is the squire?"

"I have no idea what his name is, but he saw me."

"Did he say anything?"

"Not at first, but who knows what happened when they got farther down the road. Anyway, the two of them were talking about dinner with Gawain's wife, Lady Ragnall, then he said how they had to get to the palace to let Arthur know about his sister."

"Arthur has a sister?"

"In Arthurian times, the King, Uther Pendragon, adopted a girl who would become Arthur's sister." Angelic chimes in.

"What is her name? I thought the king was missing, and why is Tristan there?"

"Morgana, and we will get to the second matter in time. She later fled the castle to join forces with a sorceress of the highest caliber."

"And she is?"

"Morgause."

"So, we can probably assume the two women you saw in your dream are Morgana and Morgause. The question is, which one is Mrs. Granada?" I look at Gwen.

Gwen's face reflects her completely lost in her own thoughts, so it doesn't surprise me when she doesn't respond. I poke her shoulder to get her attention, but she still stares blankly. I let her do her mind thing.

"So where do I come in?"

"You will need to be accompanied if you go anywhere else, Bethany. We don't need any accidents."

"A babysitter?"

"Guiney will do fine."

Bethany looks over to Gwen and me, then to Angelic. "Fine."

Bethany makes it to school in record time. Her stomach is growling, and she wants to grab a snack before class.

Heading into the school and towards the cafeteria, she hears a voice calling my name from behind.

"Bethany! You forgot to wait for me."

She turns to find Guiney running up the stairs. Bethany stands there, waiting for her to catch up. Guiney quickly stops, and a look of horror grows on her face. As her mouth opens wide, her fingers rise to point at something behind Bethany.

She turns slowly to see what exactly is making Guiney so scared and can feel the hot breath on her neck before she finishes her turn. She comes face to face with a very large lizard. It's not until its wings spread, wrapping themselves around her Bethany realizes it's no lizard.

She can hear the muffled scream coming from Guiney.

"Get Luthor!" The dragon and Bethany disappear.

My phone rings, and as I pull it out of my pocket as Gwen's begins to ring as well. "I have no idea who this is."

"Me either." We both stare at our phones.

"On three."

"One, two." Before Gwen gets to three, her phone stops ringing.

I answer mine right away. "Hello?"

I can hear a frantic voice on the other line.

"Slow down, I can't understand what you are saying." I pause, "What do you mean?" Another pause. "Oh, dear God!" One last pause. "We are on our way." I hang up.

"What is it?"

I look at her as if my puppy died. "It's Bethany."

"What about her?"

"She's been kidnapped."

"What!"

"By a dragon."

I do my best to remain calm as we fly toward the junior high. I can see Guiney in the distance, waiting for us at the top of the stairs. We come to an abrupt stop at the bottom of the stairs, and Guiney, followed by Tristan, and Mrs. Reigina join us.

"You."

Guiney walks closer to me, reaching out her arms to grab Gwen's hand. "Hello, sister."

"This whole time?"

"I am sorry I couldn't tell you sooner. I thought we had more time."

"This is not the time for explanation." Tristan chimes in.

"We must hurry." Mrs. Reigina adds as she begins to chant something too low to hear.

"Wait!"

"There is no time, Luthor!" Guiney grabs my hand to pull me in.

"No!" Gwen pulls her hand away. "What is going on?"

"We can explain on the way." Mrs. Reigina proclaims.

"Explain now! Who took Bethany? Who are you, and where the hell are we going?"

Mrs. Reigina stops her chanting long enough to answer me. "We don't know who took her, but we have an idea. My name is Lady Ragnall, and we are going to Camelot."

She doesn't give Gwen a chance to say anything else before she grabs her one hand and me with the other. The rest clasp arms, including Angelic. Lady Ragnall continues her chanting until reality fades away, and a new one materializes before us.

Welcome to Camelot!

When the vision of Camelot materializes, something inside me knows there is no way of getting out of this one.

"Welcome to Camelot." Lady Ragnall blurts suddenly. "We have no time to waste."

"What are we doing? Where do we start?"

"First things first, Luthor, you need to relax."

"You do realize who you are talking to, right Tristan?"

I look at Gwen with frustration and even though she is right, it's not funny.

"We will reconvene at my, I mean our home." Guiney includes. "No one is there, and we shouldn't be interrupted."

"So, I have a question." Gwen stops her before we continue to the home. "How are you here and there at the same time?"

"If by 'there', you mean the grade school, it's not any different than when any other spirit inhabits a being from another time."

"But, you look exactly the same. Everyone else we have ever encountered has been a different being with only similar features. How is it possible?"

"Anything can happen if you let it."

"Quoting Mary Poppins? Do you even know who she is?"

"I have been in your era long enough to know who Mary Poppins is, and I think she is wonderful."

"Enough idle chit chat." Lady Ragnall interrupts. "We must go."

The home is not very far from where we entered Camelot and is exactly how Gwen described it to us. The columns reach from floor to ceiling and every surface is covered in marble. As I pace the floor of the main room, I can't help but catch myself staring at the portrait of the family of four.

I occasionally look at it, then back to Gwen, and the similarity is uncanny. As they discuss the issues with their father, she glances at me and smiles. She doesn't have the shine in her eyes like she normally does, and it's concerning me. Is the trip back here too much? Is the memory of what happened getting to her?

My mind drifts back to the night she lost her Grams. My heart breaks even more knowing she has no one left. Oh sure, she has Bethany and I, but it's not the same. Her family is all gone, and she has no blood relatives to turn to. If she never marries another guardian, and has children, then her line will end with her, and I would hate to see it happen.

"Are you done gawking now?" Gwen comes towards me.

"Yeah. So, what is the plan?"

"Nothing I know of yet. Guinevak and I are explaining the situation with the house to Lady Ragnall and Tristan. The Lady suggested we find her husband and he can assist us."

"I know he will bring the Knights to assist us in our quest to find your sister." Lady Ragnall adds and they make their way toward Gwen and I.

"There is something you need to know before you meet anyone else." Tristan takes me by the arm and sits me down on one of the couches.

The others gather around, and by the confused expression on Gwen's face, she has no idea what he is about to say either.

"Why do you all look like you are about to tell me something horrifying?"

"Luthor, what you need to know is this, the Knights will call you by a name you are unfamiliar with." Tristan pauses for a moment, but then Guiney intervenes.

"Oh, will you get on with it? Luthor, it's believed the spirit residing in you is King Arthur himself, which is why you are here, and we believe it's why your sister has been taken."

"Impossible. I think I would know if I have some other spirit inside me."

"Would you? Gwen didn't know who she was until I pulled her here and made her see for herself."

"I didn't believe it at first either, but the proof is there." Gwen moves to my other side. "You can't deny there is a possibility."

"The question is how? How is it possible? Mom knew who she was. Why would I not?"

"I really don't know, Luthor, but I am sure there is an explanation for everything. For now, we want to warn you that the time will come when you have to find your place here." Lady Ragnall reaches for me.

"Here? What do you mean, here? You think I will be staying?"

"The decision is ultimately yours, but we hope you will allow your spirit to take its rightful place as the ruler of Camelot."

As Guiney rises, the front door of the home opens and a man in a black cloak enters. His long brown, curly hair hangs in his face, and the blue sash he wears sways when he walks.

"Let me guess, Merlin?"

"You are correct, Sire." The others look at me and I know the naming of Arthur has begun.

"What is it Merlin? Have you found out what the fire possessed? Is there magic here?" Guinevak begins to bombard him. "What information did you gain from the ashes? Do we know who is responsible?"

"Patience child and I will tell you all I know." Guinevak sits back down in the chair. "The ash I collected from the fireplace contains a mixture of nightshade, dragon's breath, and poppy flour."

"What does this mean?" Lady ponders.

"This means whoever did this was trying to cause you pain, as well as put you to sleep for a very long time. The good news is the dosage they used was not strong enough to cause the full effect they had hoped."

"It's probably why they resorted to other measures." Gwen's mind turns.

"Like taking my sister, you mean?"

"What do you mean, Sire?" Merlin seems confused. "Who is this sister you speak of?"

"Her name is Bethany, and she has been taken by a dragon and brought into this realm."

"This is most unfortunate, most unfortunate indeed." Merlin seems perplexed. "Is it possible the person who tried to poison this home also took your sister?"

"That's the idea, and I feel there are two particular people behind this, and I am afraid only magic will be able to defeat them."

"Don't be so sure." Tristan enters the conversation again. "From what I hear, the two of you are very skilled fighters."

"The way I see it, the longer we sit here gossiping, the harder it may be to find out." I get up off the couch and say the much needed words. "Out of time my sword shall find, the way to me, so I may bind."

"What is this sorcery?"

They all watch as I change in front of them. As the materials transform, I reach for the hilt of my sword. It's cold to the touch, and it feels good in my hands. When I am like this, I have a new feeling about things, more confidence, more strength, and more understanding.

As I finish transforming, the others raise and join me in a circle. "So, the plan?"

"Here is what I propose. I will venture with the Lady to the palace and we shall gather the rest of the knights. We will meet you back here in one hour. In the meantime, I suggest you gather anything you will need. Merlin, I need you to gather whatever you feel is necessary to fight dark with light. If sorcery is the only way to defeat them, then it's what it shall be."

"It will be as you say, Tristan."

"Are we agreed?" Guinevak looks to all of us.

There are a few mumbles of agreement.

"Until then, remember, one hour." Tristan heads for the door with Lady Ragnall.

I turn to Merlin, Gwen, and Guinevak, "So, it's only us then. What should we do?"

"I must get to my room to collect a few things. I see you are prepared already, but what about the two of you? Shall you fight as you are?" Merlin focuses his attention on Gwen and Guinevak.

"I will change shortly. In the meantime, I am not sure Guinevak will be fighting." Gwen begins to walk away, toward another room of the house.

"What does she mean I may not be fighting? She obviously doesn't know me."

"Um, she really doesn't."

"King or not, you aren't funny."

"Do you honestly think she will let you?"

"I didn't realize it was her decision." Guinevak storms off.

I am left standing with Merlin, and the moment becomes very awkward. I nod to him and leave the room as well.

As I move through the home I can hear the conversation about to take place. I stay hidden in the corner and watch it unfold.

Guinevak storms through the bedroom door and finds Gwen lacing up my boots. "What do you mean I won't be fighting?"

"It's simple."

"Then explain, please. I would like to know what gives you the right to tell me what I can and can't do." Guinevak places a hand on her hip and leans against the dresser. "I have fought a few times in my day and I can handle my own."

"As true as it may be, I can't rescue Bethany, protect Luthor, fend off Morgana and Morgause, and keep an eye on you. I have trained for this, have you?"

Guinevak stands in stunned silence. Her heart is already breaking at the death of her father. Gwen is only adding to the pain by speaking to her as if she is nothing more than a burden.

"Listen, you have to realize whatever life I had before I came here is unfamiliar to you. If you know how to fight, then good for you. Remember I don't know. What I do know is if something happens to you, I will never forgive myself." By now, Gwen has made my way over to Guinevak.

She knows Gwen is right, but she doesn't want to admit it. She reaches out for Gwen's hands as she approaches and makes sure her eyes show she understands.

"Come here." Gwen pulls Guinevak in. "Even though I have no memory of it, I know you are my family."

"I know."

"Then tell me you won't fight."

Guinevak pulls away slightly. "I can't. As you feel about losing me, I feel about losing you."

"Nothing will change your mind will it?"

"Nothing."

"I figured as much."

As the conversation between them ends, I move to the den and stare at the empty fireplace, feeling a chill in the air. Their father had fought his last battle in this room. Although work has been done to clean and erase the damage, the curtains have not yet been replaced. The rug is still laced with scorch marks, and the walls bear even more evidence of the damage done. As I circle around to take it all in, someone clearing their throat interrupts me. I turn around to find Tristan standing in the doorway.

"Your Majesty, we are ready when you are."

As I walk through the door, at least a dozen knights surround me. They all bow as I enter the main living room, and I do my best to bow back.

An outpouring of titled greetings overtakes me. From the simplest "Sire", to the more attention grabbing "Your Majesty". I am so taken aback by the unquestioning allegiance I feel my breath escape my chest. I straighten up from my bow and look into the faces of those who are so loyal to the person I don't even know I am. As I glance across the knights, I catch sight of Gwen and Guinevak appearing in the long hall.

Both of them walk with such admirable purpose, I am reminded I am not alone. The knights in front of me part to allow the two women to join me at my side. Without the slightest hesitation, the knights bow again to address, "Lady Guinevere". I look to Gwen and feel a surge of pride and confidence that couldn't have come from anyone else. I watch as Gwen gracefully curtsies and addresses the knights.

"Thank you for coming. We have much work ahead of us."

The knights rise to their feet once more and hold themselves in a respectful silence. It's at this moment Tristan steps forward from the ranks.

"So, what is your plan, sire?"

"First things first, we need to find where the dragon took my sister."

I get some confused looks from some of the other knights, and I know once this is all over, I will have to explain it to them.

"My lord." another knight steps up, "where would you like us to search?"

"The forest." Gwen steps up.

"My lady?"

"Do you recall the path you took with Gawain recently? The path along the stone wall?" She prompts them to think.

"Yes, my lady."

"That's where we shall begin. Gather your squires and the horses, make sure all weapons are sharp, and someone make sure Merlin has whatever he needs."

"Yes, sire."

"Men!" Lancelot shouts.

They file out of the house and I am left with Gwen, Guinevak, and an awkward feeling of being a third wheel.

Gwen is able to take us to the spot where she originally came to in her dream. As she described it, the wooden door is slightly damaged from where she hit it with her shoulder, making me wonder if it was really a dream at all. Is it possible she was transported back again when she fell asleep? If so, how did she do it on her own?

"This is it. Now remember, if they are in there they will have magic on their side. I want you to stay low and quiet until we know what we are up against."

"What of us?"

"I ask you to stay here, Guinevak, at least for now. Once we know the coast is clear, and we are able to control the situation, we will call for the three of you."

"So, you expect me to stay here?"

"Sire, your life is more important than ours. If we let you in there without knowing what to expect, we may not be prepared to protect you."

"As much as I appreciate the sentiment, I will not be standing idly by and waiting. This is my blood these women have taken, and with my blood I shall bring her back." I think for a minute and realize how the words come out. Since when do I talk like this?

"Luthor." Gwen turns to me, but I don't let her change my mind.

"I am going."

She looks at me with sad eyes and moves away, "be careful."

"Men, one at a time, and be quiet."

One by one, we file into the foliage-infested confines of the stone wall. As we enter, we divide, going in two directions. I follow to the left with Lancelot, Tristan, and five of the other knights. Gawain takes four of the others the opposite direction. As we inch closer to what we think is the center, a low moaning reaches our ears. The nature of it's unclear, but whatever is causing it, doesn't sound human.

Instead of following along the wall, I motion for the men to aim towards the center. We fan out into a line and slowly make our way inward. Within a few feet, I can see what is making the noise. It's larger than I expected it to be, and it looks peaceful as it sleeps.

The scales of the dragon shimmer in the sunlight. Its deep purple coloring fades to a midnight black as the scales become less thick on its limbs. Its muscular body connects to a thick neck and a long tail, and the end of the tail is endowed with a hook-like protrusion. The dragon's elongated limbs each end with three splayed digits on each foot with long, blunt claws. It has ragged-looking wings running from its shoulders to the middle of its tail, while its small mouth hides multiple rows of teeth. A mane of bony spikes sprouts from the back of its head, and a series of tentacle-like tendrils protrude from its chin. As it blinks awake, its scarlet colored eyes shine in the light.

Raising its head and tilting from one side to the other, the spikes on the top sways with every turn. When it rises onto its front legs, I can see a small person with red hair curled on the stone. I want to scream her name, but I know we must stay quiet.

I can see the other group across the way and I signal for them to stand down. As we wait patiently to see the dragon's next move, two new figures come into view. I glare towards Gawain, but before we can act, a rustling comes from between us.

We all turn our heads to see Merlin making his way down the center path. He is cloaked with his staff in hand. Around his waist are a few bottles filled with different liquids and powders. His lips are moving, and he speaks words only he can hear.

As he approaches the stone altar, the two figures turn, and I realize they are women. These are probably the same from Gwen's dream. Both have long, dark hair. One of them has hair curly as moss, the other is as straight as can be. Both wear red corseted bodices and pitch-black cloaks. Their hoods are down, and their hands are exposed.

Before Merlin can react, a ball of fire flies from the hands of one of the women and slams into his chest. He is knocked backwards, but he doesn't fall. Laughing, he wipes away the soot.

"I thought you were a mighty sorceress, Morgause? Tell me there is more to you."

"You may play smart, but you lack the power to defeat me."

"We shall see."

He pauses briefly and turns to face where I stand. He nods his head, and I come out of hiding, motioning for the rest to stay behind. As I stand next to him, he slips a bottle to me, doing his best to keep the witches' attention on him. I place the bottle in my back pocket and we separate slightly.

A smirk grows on Morgause's face as she realizes who I am. "Our precious king has come home at last."

Both women laugh together, and I can see Bethany squirming in her chains behind them. "Leave him alone you horrid beasts."

Morgana whips around to face Bethany. "Such distaste from such a lovely creature. You should save those words." She raises her arms to reach towards Bethany and speaks, "Silentium."

Bethany falls silent, but her body continues to move. Her aggravation escalates as it becomes apparent her words can't escape her lips. Bethany flails around to the best of her ability, making absolutely sure the witches know how angry she is.

"Will you sit still?" Morgana screams.

Suddenly, Bethany falls limp onto the slab.

"No!" I make a dash for her.

Morgause points a finger at me, and I feel my feet slowly rise from the ground. She raises her hand towards the sky, causing my body to seize. I try to move my arms, but I am frozen. I can hear Merlin making his way closer, and he is mumbling something again. With every word coming out of his mouth, I lower inch by inch. You can see pain growing in Morgause's devilish brown eyes.

Tension grows, and her teeth clench. I look over towards the other woman and realize she has begun her own chanting. She is facing the direction in which I know Merlin stands. As soon as I get the movement in my head back, I turn to him. His face is growing pale, and he slows in his steps.

"Merlin!"

"The vial!"

"I still can't move my arms."

Being distracted by myself and Merlin, the two witches don't see the knights moving in behind them. The dragon, however, is very aware of their movement. Dropping from its perch, the dragon lands behind the slab and raises its head high. It opens its mouth and clenches the muscles in its large neck, while it summons its own magical fire to bring to the fight. As the flame begins to crackle inside its wide-open mouth, the knights draw their shields. Covering their bodies, they barely protect themselves from the blast.

As the dragon attacks the knights from the front, the rest of our fighting forces get behind the dragon. While it's distracted, Gawain goes to save Bethany, and sparks fly as Gawain's sword clashes against Bethany's bonds, but they don't break.

"They are probably enchanted! It won't be easy."

"Quiet! I am not finished with you yet." Morgause lashes out at me.

Finally, my feet connect with the solid ground. The combat is taking its toll on Morgause and Merlin. Morgause's body is looking worn, but the other woman looks like nothing is phasing her.

I twist around to check on Merlin and notice his face growing pale and weak. "Merlin!"

He turns his droopy eyes towards me, and I can see he is suffering from the great pain being put on him. "The vial."

With all of my movement back, I reach for the vial in my back pocket.

"Throw it." His voice is strained.

I throw it as hard as I can in Morgause's direction. It breaks at her feet and a puff of lavender smoke emanates from the ground. She covers her mouth as she begins to cough from inhaling the fumes. It gives enough time for Merlin to regain his own composure and throw another vial at Morgana's feet. A similar puff of smoke rises, the color of amber surrounds her, and the smell alone brings her to her knees.

"No!" Morgause screams as she raises her arms, her fingers protruding forward, but nothing happens. "What is this?" Raising her arms again trying to cast a spell, nothing happens.

"We only have a few seconds before it wears off."

"What do we do?"

"We fight."

I draw my sword and advance towards Morgause. She pulls a dagger from between her breasts and catches my blow at the right time. Merlin doesn't carry any weapons, and I can't concentrate on what he is doing.

Morgause strikes towards my right shoulder and catches me with the tip of her blade. I flinch backward and swing the sword at her abdomen. Instead of cutting her, it hits her and bounces off her skin. As she begins to laugh, she places the dagger back in her dress.

With a snap of her fingers, she begins to dissipate into thin air. "Morgana!"

Morgana dodges Merlin's reach and drops something to the ground. Glass shatters and she leaves in a cloud of red smoke, with Merlin and I perplexed.

"Why would they leave?" I notice heat is emanating from behind me.

Merlin and I turn our attention to the dragon. I look at him briefly as the knights are doing their best to free Bethany and fend off the dragon at the same time. Lowering his head, Merlin begins another incantation. "Liberum, et vincula solvere haec anima tua, abscide eam, et vincula tua." He raises his hands towards Bethany and lets go a breath of relief when the chains break away.

Gawain helps her off the altar as the rest of the knights are concentrating on the dragon. "Get her out of here."

"Sire?"

"Now!" As he whisks her away, I call to the others, "Retreat, men, retreat!"

I stand there and watch as the men slowly back away toward the entrance. I glare at Merlin to let him know he, too, has to go. I know I can't be responsible for putting the rest of their lives in danger now Bethany is safe. He returns my gaze with despair. It's as if he feels I will not make it out alive. Instead of saying anything, I shake my head and nod for him to go. Before he turns to leave, he whispers something to himself.

When he is finished, I can feel a heavy weight pull on my body. I look down and I am covered in armor, a leather jerkin worthy of a king. On my head is a golden helmet, with a crest carved in the shape of a dragon. Across my shoulders a circular shield materialized, with a painted likeness of the Blessed Mary. I hold my sword at my side, and I brace myself for a fight.

As they exit the battlefield, the dragon turns its attention toward me. I dive for the altar and curl up in a ball, out of sight. Waiting and listening, I do my best to get a feel for where the dragon is. Crawling on my knees, I make my way around the stone altar, looking up to find the dit facing the other way. It huffs in anger, knowing its prize has been stolen.

I get up as quietly as I can. Raising the sword, I swing desperately at the dragon, but the blade bounces harmlessly off the great beast's scales. The dragon rears its head and I can see its nostrils flare. Before it can release its fiery fury, I drop into a small crevice in the rock behind me. The dragon flaps its wings, raising itself off the ground. As it comes toward me, it roars and scrapes at the entrance, but avoids me all together.

I catch my breath and grip my sword again. Before the dragon can swipe at the entrance a third time, I roll out under its paw, and drive my sword through its padding. It lets out a deafening growl and flaps its wings harder.

I try to pull the sword out, but the more it flaps its wings, the harder it's to hold on. As the sword slips through my fingers, I grip it with both hands and pull with everything I have. The sword breaks free, and the dragon hollers again.

With me in its sights, it rises high into the air, stops for a second, and dives towards me. As it gets closer, I can see the flames building inside its mouth. Before I can dive out of the way, I hear the whistle of an arrow flying past my head and straight into the dragon's lower jaw. Another arrow shoots straight through its wing.

I turn to see Gwen a few feet away. "You didn't think I was going to let you have all the fun, did you?"

She reaches for my arm and helps me to my feet. By now, the dragon has turned its back to the stone altar and is lying there whimpering. Blood is slowly dripping from the wound in its mouth and paw. "I can't bring myself to finish it off." I gaze at Gwen.

"It's the beast that took your sister. If you leave it to live, how do you know it won't be any more of a problem?"

"I don't, but think about it this way, it's acting under direction from someone else. Like you said, it was created from a bird."

I turn toward the dragon. With everything that is happening, I want to be angry, but I simply am not.

"Maybe you are right."

Another figure approaches from behind the stone altar. She doesn't pay any attention to the fact we are there, but focuses her attention on the dragon.

I look at Gwen and she stands in awe. "Oh wow."

"Who is it?"

Gwen doesn't answer right away, so I turn my attention back to the woman in white. She is not much taller than I am, and her long curly brown hair stands piled on her head. She has the brightest blue eyes, and the dress she wears fits her like a glove. It's best described as off white and has small circular mirrors along her stomach. The top half only covers enough to not show off anything important, and it flows down to her feet as she walks.

She glances up at Gwen, but never says a word. She gets closer to the dragon and begins to caress its spiked head. As she does, she whispers something to it, causing it to close its eyes. The dragon's breathing slows, and you can see it relaxing.

"This beast has seen enough torment from Morgause and Morgana. Leave it in peace and it shall leave you the same."

"It took my sister."

"My lord, you have to understand something; not all things are the way they seem."

"What do you mean?"

"This is not the creature who took her. He is only the one to guard her."

"I am lost."

She makes her way around the stone and converges on Gwen and I. As she gets closer, I can see Gwen out of the corner of my eye, placing her right foot forward and slowly lowering the top half of her body. Why is she bowing? Before I can get an answer, Gwen grabs my arm and pulls me down with her. I turn my head towards her, furrow my brow, and glare. She gives me a look and raises back up.

"Forgive me, my lady."

"It's alright, young guardian." The lady makes her way towards Gwen. "You have always been such a beauty." She places her hands on Gwen's face.

"Thank you, my lady."

"You, sire, I think are more astute to the situation."

I tilt my head and give her a questioning look. "I am not sure I understand what you mean."

"My lady, you must forgive him, he is not as aware as we hoped, but he is getting there."

"I see." She turns away from us and goes back to the dragon.

She runs her hand along the scales of its paw and it whimpers in pain. Leaning forward, she blows on the wound I gave it with my sword only a few moments before. I watch as the opening begins to heal, and the blood disappears. She makes her way to the other side and brushes its snout. While we watch, the woman whispers to it again. The dragon lowers its head and without warning, she grasps the arrow and pulls it from the jaw. It doesn't roar, growl, or get angry, it just lifts its head, whimpers a little, and rests it back down again. Like the paw, the hole begins to close, and the blood begins to disappear.

When she finishes, she whispers one more thing to it. It begins to raise itself up and flaps its enormous wings. Bursts of air blow at us as it rises higher and higher into the air. Within moments, it's only a spec in the sky.

"Why did you let it go?"

"It has a name, and it's Balderon."

"How do we know it won't harm anyone else?"

"I don't. We will have to trust it will follow the path I have led it on."

"Is that what you were saying?"

"Yes, my queen."

"You speak draconic?"

"I speak many languages, Guinevere. Now I must go. You have a mission to complete." She looks from Gwen to me. "Take care of the sword, for it's your life."

She breaks apart into the air and is gone. I look back to Gwen, then to the spot where the lady stood, then back to Gwen again. She is laughing at me because she knows I have no idea who that was.

Walking towards me, she reaches out her arm, wraps it around my shoulder. "You really should read more."

"I guess so." We make our way to meet the others outside the stone wall. "So, are you going to tell me who it was?"

"Nope."

I think I overslept...

The next morning, I awake to find Gwen standing over me. She doesn't look happy and because it's so early, I have no idea what I did wrong this time. I bring myself up on my elbows and look her dead in the eye. "What time is it?"

"Seven o'clock, now get up." She grabs the blanket and gives it a good yank. It's wrapped in between my legs so as the blanket goes to the floor, so do I.

Landing with a thump, I am up enough to now know what she is upset about. I was supposed to relieve her at five o'clock. This means either she fell asleep and woke up realizing what time it's or stayed awake the whole time.

"Neither."

"What?"

"Bethany relieved me about four, so I could get some sleep. She is in the living room right now standing guard."

"Wait, did you?"

"No, I didn't read your mind dork, you don't whisper softly." She turns away and heads for the door.

"Oh, I thought I said it in my head."

"Nope." She slams the door behind her.

"Whoops."

I make good time getting dressed and meeting them in the living room. At least I think it's everyone. Gwen is not there, and Guinevak has gone to the kitchen to get something to drink.

"It's about time you decided to join us."

"Sorry sis, I must have been more tired than I thought. Did Gwen go get some rest?" I sit down on the couch next to her.

"Yes."

"Has anyone come to the house since last night?"

"No. Why don't you get something to eat? I'll be fine. I'll call if I need anything."

I pass Guinevak carrying a tray of food as I head towards the kitchen. She gives me a glare, and I know this is not going to be a fun morning.

Guinevak brings the tray of food and sets it on the small marble table in front of Bethany. Eyeing the tray, she has no real desire to eat anything. Her mind is still reeling over the last day or so and what happened with the dragon. "Do you want to talk about it?"

"Not really, Guinevak."

"Ok. I'll sit here and watch with you then." Guinevak turns and smiles, even though her sarcasm is not appreciated.

Sitting with her arms crossed, and her legs up on the coffee table, Bethany contemplates the ordeals and fights back the urge to spill about everything happening, but she can't. She is still upset with Guiney for not telling her the truth the whole time they were friends. Has she always been Guinevak? Why would she not tell Bethany?

"I know what you are thinking."

"You honestly have no idea." Bethany continues to look the other way, avoiding all eye contact.

"You are wondering why I didn't tell you. You are wondering how long I was portraying Guiney, and whether or not I am actually your friend or playing a part. Listen, I can answer all your questions, but will it matter? Is it going to change the way you feel about me right now?"

"No, but it will at least give me answers."

"So be it. You can be mad at me all you want, but I have reasons and they are good. I can tell you or I can't, it's up to you." Guinevak grabs a piece of cheese and bread off the tray and raises from the couch.

As she makes her way towards the den, she can hear Bethany squirm behind her. Guinevak goes into the den to pull a few books from her father's bookshelf.

As she stands there gliding along the leather spines, dust collects on her fingertips. Every few books, she blows the dust off and gives a little cough. "Where is it, where it's, where it's?"

"Where is what?" Guinevak turns to find Bethany standing in the doorway.

"A special book my father used to read to me. Now he is gone, I want to make sure I hide it before the home gets taken away from me."

"What do you mean?"

"When my father passed, he had no boys. When this happens, the land goes to the crown since it's theirs to begin with."

"Well, since they think Luthor is the king, can't he do something about it?"

"I am not sure. I haven't brought it up."

"I will." Bethany turns to confront Luthor about it.

"No."

"Why not? If he is the king and I am his sister, then there is no reason for him not to listen."

"I have a plan."

"What?"

"I will marry a knight and become a lady of the court; presumably a lady to the queen."

"What happens if it fails?"

"It won't fail because she is not going anywhere. She will stay where she is until she chooses to leave, and she will have all the same comforts as before."

"As you wish, sire."

Gwen sits in her room contemplating the findings of the last few days. She has so much running through her mind it will not allow her to get any more rest. Why did the lady of the lake let the dragon go? Does Luthor seriously not know who she is?

"Man doesn't know his own shadow." She rolls over to her side and closes her eyes, and finally falls asleep.

She is standing in front of her bedroom door. Someone is knocking lightly, but she can't move. "My lady?" A woman's voice calls from the other side. "My lady, are you there?" The woman then jiggles the locked handle.

Gwen reaches for the handle, but her hand goes right through it. "What is this? What is going on?"

Before she can find an answer, a rustling comes from behind me. She turns to face a memory from the past, a dream from when they were on Olympus. The problem is, it's not a new dream, it's the same one with a twist.

"You!"

"It isss I."

There is a fear Gwen has felt before as she stares at the beast of a woman. "What do you want?"

"You have taken sssomething from me, now I will take sssomething from you."

"What have I taken?"

"Everything." Echidna lunges at Gwen.

She reaches for the bow but is not fast enough. Echidna brings down a clawed hand across Gwen's arm. Four long gashes seep red liquid as she tries to steady herself.

Echidna rears back and goes to strike again. This time reaching for her bow, Gwen places an arrow in her abdomen. There is a high-pitched screech followed by a long hiss. "You will regret this."

"I owe you nothing!"

"You took away my child, now I will take away yoursss!"

"I will not pay for the actions of her sister!"

"Your sssissster? You have no sssissster."

"You know so little."

Suddenly, Guinevak comes through the door; "Sister." she calls out, "catch".

Gwen suddenly catches a wrapped figure. It almost slips through her arms, but she is able to hold on to it. Looking down, she sees the face of a child, but this child is different. This child has scales instead of skin, and beady red eyes.

"Did you?"

"Give her back!" Guinevak calls from the doorway.

Gwen drifts towards the Echidna holding out the infant. "Here, take it."

"It's not so easssy. You ssstill sssstole my child."

Echidna lunges as Guinevak dives in and pushes Gwen away. Losing her balance, Echidna falls to the ground, the arrow completely pushing its way through. She lets out a quiet squeal as she begins to roll to her side. "My child, my child."

Gwen moves slowly as she brings the child closer. "It's right here."

"Bring her to me, pleassse."

Guinevak moves to the other side to face the woman. "Echidna, I didn't steal your child, I promise."

"I don't believe you."

"I." Guinevak reaches for the child. "She was found in an old quarry in modern times. No one knows how she got there or why. She was given to me by the person who found her."

"Who gave her to you?" Echidna's words are barely audible by now.

"The queen of Camelot."

"The what?" Gwen calls out.

"The queen mother. She was exploring San Diego to keep an eye on Luthor when she came across the child in a quarry." Guinevak hands Echidna the child. "She brought her back here and gave her to me for safe keeping until we could figure out what to do."

"Who would do this?"

"I'm not sure, Gwen."

"There isss only one who would dare."

"Who?"

"Herculesss."

"Why would he?"

"To dessstroy me." Echidna coughs slightly, almost losing the grip on the child.

"We need to get you help." Guinevak gets to her feet.

"It isss too late now." Echidna lowers her head, and her eyes close.

"No!" Guinevak drops back to her knees.

The child's eyes are closed as well. Gwen reaches for it and wraps it in her arms. As she begins to stroke the tiny green scales on the child's face, she realizes it's not breathing. A gasp catches her, and Guinevak knows as well.

"What do we do now?" Guinevak rises again.

"We give them the burial they deserve."

"But they aren't from this time."

"It doesn't matter. They deserve a proper burial, and we will give it to them. Fetch the gardener, the physician, and a few of the men we can trust."

Gwen wakes to find herself covered in sweat and her cheeks are crusted over from tears. Pulling herself up in bed, she recounts the moments in the dream. The question is, was it really a dream? "This is getting ridiculous." She begins to retreat from the bed feet first. As she moves her arm, she can feel the aftermath of the scratches like a ghost limb feels an itch.

She goes over the moments in her head as she gets dressed. '*First it's the visions when I touch something, now I am experiencing things in my dream that seem so real. Is this some kind of new power? Is this part of the trials? If it's, why didn't I get some kind of notice like the first one?*'

Before she continues her thoughts, there is a knock on the door. "Come in."

The door creaks, and he peeks his head in. "I am really going to have someone do something about the noise this door makes."

She continues to get her boots on and doesn't respond to my comment. I make my way into the room and take a brief look around. Each room seems to have its own theme though. Mine looks to be more based on subtle luxury; ya know, basic but elegant. The room Gwen is in has tons of flowers everywhere, and was definitely meant for a girl. Come to think of it, I wonder if I am sleeping in Guinevak's room.

"What do you want?"

"Still mad at me; got it."

"Shouldn't I be? It's bad enough you don't relieve me when you are supposed to, but now I barely get any sleep and these dreams are becoming a nightmare." She goes to a closet and pulls out a long brown cape. It ties in the front and the hood is trimmed with a light gold threading.

As she flings it around her back, it lifts in the air like a wave rippling in the ocean. If you watch it in slow motion, you'd swear it was magic.

"What dreams? Did you have another one?" I reach out to her, but she pulls away.

"Yes. It was the snake dream again, but this time it was longer." She moves past me and heads for the door.

"What happened?" I reach for her again as she walks past, but again she pulls away. Before she can make it to the door, I scream to her, "Hey!" She turns to face me. "Whatever I did, I am sorry. It's not like I did it on purpose. Whatever is going on with you lately, you can stop acting like I am this horrible person and maybe talk to me, ya know, as we used to. What happened to us? Is this how our friendship is going to be? First the outburst in Milady D'Winter's house, and now the whole cold shoulder thing? Is oversleeping so big of an issue you have to be like this?"

I wait for a response, but it never comes. Instead, her eyes fill with tears. Before she lets one drop, she turns away and leaves the room. I don't let her get far, but before I can reach her, Bethany comes out of another room to her right and stops me. Gwen makes her way down the hall leaving Bethany and I alone.

"Let her go."

"Why? I am not going to be the bad guy here because I overslept." I yank my arm from her grasp.

"You really are as clueless as you seem, aren't you? Have you never paid attention in school? How do you pass anything?" Bethany becomes irate with me.

"I am not stupid, of course I paid attention, but it doesn't mean I am a genius who knows everything."

"King Arthur, think about it. How does the story end?"

"Oh god! There has to be more than that though. She has been acting like this on and off for a while now."

I gasp as I think about it. I have read none of the books, but I know from enough movies King Arthur always dies in the end. Guinevere always leaves and goes to a convent.

"Exactly, now think about how she is feeling, knowing the story can play itself out like it always does."

"She thinks I am going to die? Is that why she is acting like this?"

"Color me impressed, he gets it."

"Not funny."

"Go to her, take her in the den, sit her down, and talk to her. This time don't be all Mr. Angry Pants about it. Show her you understand and reassure her it will not turn out the way she thinks." Bethany begins to walk down the hall, but my words stop her.

"But what if it does happen?"

"Make sure it doesn't." She leaves me standing in the hallway as she makes her way to the others.

I wait a few moments before following behind where I find Gwen, Guinevak, and Bethany sitting around the living area talking. Guinevak holds a book in her hands, and they are discussing what to do about the house. I stand quietly behind the couch so as to not interrupt their conversation. When they realize I am there, I catch Gwen's attention and motion with my head for her to join me in the den.

She stands up reluctantly and doesn't say a word to me as she makes her way through the double doors. I follow her in and shut them behind me as I enter. A light click sounds as the latch locks us in, leaving us to be uninterrupted.

Her back is to me, and I can tell she is tense. She has a way she stands when things are weighing her down. Her shoulders will slump, her head will be lower, and she always bends her right knee. She will ring her hands like she is massaging them, and every so often she will turn her head from side to side to stretch her neck.

Walking up behind her, I catch her in mid-stretch and place my hands on her shoulders. I only get in a second or two of massaging when she pulls away from me with a jerk of her shoulder and makes her way to a chaise lounge in the corner. I stand for a moment watching her, waiting for a signal to move forward. When the signal doesn't come, I go to her anyway. Every time she wants to push me away, I keep following behind. Now I know what is bothering her, I am not going to let her deal with it without knowing I understand.

I sit down next to her and as she tries to get up, I grab her by the arm and pull her back down. She plops to the seat and gives a slight oomph as she makes contact with the leather cushion. "Can you let me go, please?"

"No."

"You are hurting my arm." She begins to try and twist out of my grip.

"Not until you stop avoiding me and either tell me what it's or listen to what I have to say."

She stops wiggling for a minute and I release her arm. We sit in silence as I wait to see if she is going to talk to me about it or not.

"No."

"No, what?"

She looks at me, and her eyes are sad, sadder than I have ever seen them before. "I won't lose you."

I grab her hand and inch closer. "You won't"

She shakes her head, and a tear drops to her leg. "I know how the story ends."

"It's only a story."

"It's your life."

"This is not going to be an argument I will win is it?"

She looks down shyly, but sadly. "Probably not."

"Then I guess I will have to prove you wrong instead."

"That's a first."

"Is this a challenge?"

Instead of answering me, she wraps her arms around my shoulders and squeezes as hard as she can. I turn the top half of my body towards her and return her embrace. She has a point, and I know some people say you can control fate, but can you really?

Guinevak and Bethany sit quietly in the living area, Bethany staring off blankly while Guinevak reads from the book. She hasn't spoken since she was taken by the dragon, and she is dying to talk to someone about it. Guinevak will occasionally shift her body, or look off at Bethany, but never says a word. Is she ignoring her, or is she seriously engrossed in the book? She looks up and Guinevak returns the gaze.

"You have been squirming like a fish out of water for almost an hour. What is it? Are you getting antsy?" Guinevak chuckles.

Bethany takes it as a sign she is ok to listen to her story now. She excitedly moves to the end of the couch, closer to Guinevak. Pulling her feet in behind her, she places her arms on the arm of the couch and stares.

"What? I am waiting."

Bethany stares at her with a cheesy grin growing bigger and bigger by the second.

"You are ridiculous." Guinevak goes back to her book. She is only a few sentences in when Bethany finally speaks.

"Ok, so." Before she can go on, Gwen and I come from the den and join them.

"Story time?"

"Shh, I am just getting started, Luthor."

"Ok, ok."

"Ok, where was I?"

"At the beginning."

"It's a very good place to start." Gwen chuckles.

"Really, you too? I'd expect it from him, but not you."

"So, who wants to hear a story about a dragon? Fine then. So, Guiney and I were walking into school. I was ahead of her, and it was when Guiney saw it first. I didn't really get a good look at it, but its breath was definitely hot on my neck. I could see the fear in Guiney's eyes, and before I knew what happened, I was whooshed away. I woke up a short time later, in a stone place where you found me. I was not sure how long I had been there, but no one ever came or went. The dragon was guarding me, well, you saw what it looked like; big, scaly, spiky hair. It was wrapped around me sleeping, and I could move around it, but I couldn't escape because of the chains. Here is the kicker though; the dragon guarding me was not the same one that took me.

I knew by the smell. The smell coming off the thing that took me was more like burned wood. The one watching over me smelled more of a mixture of scents like flowers and sulfur. They handled me differently too. The dragon that took me was rougher with deeper and sharper claws. The one protecting me seemed gentler and subdued. So my theory is this, they took me because of you." She points to me.

"We caught that part I am sure."

"What I don't understand is why the dragon didn't hurt me; neither of them."

"Do you want to hear my theory?" Guinevak intervenes.

"Sure."

"It's because they need you. Here is my theory. They kidnapped you because you are his majesty's sister. I do believe they are two different creatures. From what I remember of the moment you were taken, the creature that took you didn't resemble a dragon. Being all black, its wingspan was not as large and wide as one. The wings themselves were more sheer, too. Most dragons have a thicker wing density. Then there was the body of the creature; it seemed almost human. Its legs and arms were shaped like you or me, but black like the creature's color. Lastly, the scales were all off. They only covered about ninety percent of its body instead of the whole thing."

"So where does your theory come in?"

"My theory is the creature who took you is not a creature at all, but a manifestation created by someone with magic, or, it was the person themselves, transformed temporarily into the creature to bring you here, then have the dragon itself guard you." Guinevak sits back, feeling proud of herself.

"A very good theory, and one we plan to soon classify as reality." The deep male voice breaks into the conversation. I turn to face him, and he bows to me. "My lord."

"Tell us what you have found."

Tristan sits opposite me on the couch. He leans forward, placing his elbows on his knees. "My lord."

"Call me Luthor for now, please."

"Yes my, Luthor. As I was saying, we combed the town to find any sign of Morgana and Morgause but found nothing. Merlin is now, as we speak, in his chambers preparing a potion we believe will subdue their powers and allow us to capture them. The only downfall is we need to find them and get close enough to deliver it to them."

"Will the rest be joining us?"

"Shortly, my queen."

Gwen looks at me with questionable eyes. *'my queen'* she lips to me. I shrug, unknowing why he would call her that.

"So be it. For now, we will prepare ourselves."

They all look at me as if to wonder why I get the last word.

That's some castle...

We decide instead of having everyone join us at the house, we will go to the castle instead. Guinevak and Bethany stay in the middle, Gwen and I take the front, and Tristan flanks us, staying in this formation through the whole ride.

As we approach, it's not as I expected. To tell you the truth, I was not sure what to expect. It's surrounded by a moat spanning a hundred feet or so from the ground to the castle itself. Two large towers hug the front two corners, and two smaller ones frame the gate. There is no drawbridge, but there is a small stone watchman's shack centered on the path. There are about twenty windows showing in the front, too small for anyone to really fit through.

You can see two long stacks near the back, and I wonder what they are for. They don't look wide enough to be rooms, but maybe cells for prisoners. The stone itself was once tan, but you can tell time has aged it. Most of it's turning to a dark gray and chipping away. About halfway from the grounds to the castle lay a wooden bridge, while the other half turns into a small island-like path of stone and grass.

We ride single file until we all make it through the rusty, iron gate. As the last of us come through, they lower it down again. I am greeted with a slew of welcomes, and your majesty's. It's all I can do to keep up with the nodding back to them. Servants and peasants alike line the pathway of the courtyard. A few stable hands take the horses as we dismount, Tristan barking orders to have them watered, fed and brushed.

The Knights of the Round Table meet us by the main entrance, standing single file. As we approach, Gwen tells me their names.

"I know you have met them already, technically."

"I don't know all their names though."

"Follow my lead. The first one is Geraint."

"Which one?"

"The one on the far left."

"Then?"

"Percival, Bors, Lamorak, Kay, Gareth, Bedivere, Gaheris, Galahad, and of course you know Tristan, Gawain, and Lancelot."

"Gentleman."

"Sire."

I examine them all for a moment. They look so regal and well kept. For most of them, their hair is long and tied back, but a few others have shorter hair. They all wear tall black boots, puffy white shirts, and chain mail hoods. Some of their tunics are different though. Some have white tunics with a red cross. Some have red tunics with a white cross, and some wear no tunic at all.

"Your majesty, should we adjourn to the Round Table?"

"Please, call me Luthor."

The knight's part down the middle as I pass. We make our way through a long corridor until we come to a large room. As we enter, the table is the first thing I see, sitting dead center of the room. There are easily twenty-five high back wooden seats, but Gwen has only mentioned about eleven or twelve to me. Who are the rest?

Before my question is answered, everyone starts to gather around the table. Gwen takes a seat in a low red velvet lined chair at one side of the table, and Bethany takes a seat next to her. I can tell by the way the table is laid out, I have my place too. There is a painting of a man who looks like me on the wall behind the largest chair. I take it as my seat and make my way there, resting in front of Gwen and Bethany. Lady Ragnall takes a seat not far from where Gawain stands, and a few servants spread out around us. None of them sit, and before I can say anything, they all draw their swords and place them along the table in front of them; points to the center. As I examine the table closer, it reminds me of a roulette wheel. Every other section is painted white or a dark red. The inner edge is trimmed in green, the outer edge is white, and the names of the knights are written where they stand. The center, painted with a red flower, has white petals in the center and a yellow bud in the middle. It too is surrounded by a white border with something written on it.

Within seconds of them placing their swords, they all start speaking in unison.

"To never do outrage nor murder. Always to flee treason. To by no means be cruel but to give mercy unto him who asks for mercy. To always do ladies, gentlewomen and widows succor. To never force ladies, gentlewomen or widows. Not to take up battles in wrongful quarrels for love or worldly goods. This is our vow, this is our oath." When they finish, they pull their chairs out and sit.

Suddenly the doors come open and Merlin enters the room. Without saying a word, he takes a seat opposite me, but not at the table. He nods politely, and I return the gesture. I decide since he is our magic expert, I will start with what he has to say.

"Merlin, if you please." I raise my hand for him to step forward. "Tell us what we have."

"Sire, I have dug through everything I have. I believe I have developed a potion to subdue their powers permanently."

"This is good news."

"Yes, sire. It's a binding spell, which contains purified water, a whole white rose, mustard seed, sea salt, anise, bat guano."

I raise my hand for him to stop. "I get it. How do you plan on administering it to them?"

"Might be a little more difficult. We have to get them into a position leaving them helpless; a battle perhaps."

The knights begin pounding on the table.

He sits back down, and I look over to Lancelot. "What is the knight's plan for finding them?

"Divide and conquer, sire."

"Divide and conquer?"

"Yes, sire. We have enough men that we can scour the area for them. We will divide in groups of three and go from town to town until we find them."

"What happens when you do find them?" Gwen speaks up.

"We will call for the others."

"How?"

"By hawk."

"By hawk?"

"Curtis, your majesty."

I look at Gwen again after he says it, and she gives me another look of confusion. "I see."

"And then what?" I continue.

"We will regroup and converge on them."

"How much do we know about them and their powers?" Bethany speaks next.

Merlin steps up again and begins telling us a story. "Morgause is the self-absorbed, narcissistic, self-indulgent Queen of Lothian and Orkney. She was married to Lot before he was killed by Pellinore."

"And my disowned mother." Gawain intervenes.

"We refer to her in the magic world as the Queen of Air and Darkness. Some think she is not smart enough to be a serious sorceress. I have been told much of her witchcraft is done out of boredom, which can be dangerous. Be afraid. Be terrified." His voice trembles slightly.

"What about Morgana, my half-sister?" I add in air quotes.

"She disowned your father, took Morgause as her sister, and has been taught the ways of sorcery."

"Why has nothing been done about this before?"

"It has never been a major threat until now, sire."

"Ok, first things first, please stop with the sire and majesty. My name is Luthor; call me Luthor. Secondly, it seems hard to believe. How long ago did she disown him?"

"Just before his death."

"And that was?" Everyone gasps at my question. "Seriously, you all forget I am here as Luthor, not Arthur, so if I should know something, you are going to have to tell me."

"Two years ago." Tristan finally answers.

"So, two years ago, why?"

"Because she betrayed him."

"How?"

"This is a long story, Luthor. I hope you have the time for me to tell it." Merlin tries to persuade me to move on.

"Tell me anyway."

"The relationship between Uther and Morgana was a strained one. He did care for her, but was too proud to tell her he was her father. However, I am sure there are other reasons for not revealing this to her. She was and is a supporter of magic, and it's what put them at odds with each other. I think he secretly knew she was a witch but didn't want to admit it to himself. Morgana hid a Druid boy Uther was trying to locate once, and he told her he will not hesitate to break the promise he made to Gorlois if she ever betrayed him again. From that moment on, Uther kept his promise and his feelings began to soften towards her. However, it didn't take long for Morgana to side with our enemies and stopped seeing Uther as her family.

After Morgana was reportedly kidnapped by Morgause, Uther's obsession with finding her nearly destroyed his army after sending them on repeated searches. It was not until I cast a spell making Morgana fall down a flight of stairs and becoming badly wounded that he revealed his true relationship to her. Morgana became enraged Uther never told her the truth about her heritage and thought he cared more about his own reputation than he did about her.

Uther discovered Morgana's treachery when she proceeded to torture him by forcing him to witness her slaughter innocent people. She claimed to be mirroring his own actions, and she was going to execute him once she was done torturing him. Morgause came to the kingdom with her army, and Uther was thrown into the dungeons.

About a year later, her betrayal broke him to the point of weakness in the mental and physical state, making him unfit to rule. He didn't show signs of improvement until your birthday, when he protected you from an assassin attempt and became mortally wounded. She willingly caused your father's death by enchanting a necklace reversing any healing spell and worsening the ailment tenfold. She is now in full league with Morgause and together they are a terrible duo to control."

I sit in stunned silence, never hearing this before. I look around at the table and those sitting outside of it and know by their sad and grim faces the story is difficult to hear. I rise, realizing someone has brought us drinks. Picking up the glass, I raise it into the air and call for a toast. "To Uther!"

I am returned with a slew of 'long live the king', 'to his majesty', and 'to Uther.' I lower the glass without drinking from it and sit back down. "So, something was technically attempted, but never carried to completion. We must execute a plan perfectly, otherwise it will be for not. Here is what I propose, you will divide into groups of four, and no less. You will take to places where no one would normally look. I want you to check back at the confines where we regained my sister as well. If it's one of the main places they hide, they will go back there. The rest of us will stay here and guard the castle. The remaining knights will guard the surrounding walls high above the moat. I want archers stationed every few feet. All servants and peasants not fighting will need to gather anything they need and head to safety. I don't want any innocent people being harmed in this. For now, we will eat and rest; tomorrow it begins." Everyone applauds, and we disperse to another part of the castle to eat.

The great hall is three times the size of the room the Round Table is in. It's easily big enough to fit five hundred or more people. Seven long wooden tables line the room., each one using benches to sit.

There is already an array of foods on the table, ranging from a hog to a few plucked birds. Different platters fill the empty spaces with things like grapes, figs, pears, nuts, cheese and bread. Every few feet there is a pitcher of wine or some kind of beer or mead, as the knights call it, and I know better than to partake. Even though I am technically the king, in my world I am still underage.

There are no tablecloths or silverware, but there are some burlap looking runners on them. Every so often, you will find a floral arrangement with a candelabra in the center. With all the candles going, it brightens up what would normally be a very dark room. The ceilings are high, and instead of being ornate or fancy, it's a simple flat ceiling made of stone and wood framing. Like the outside, the stone is turning gray and chipping away. I don't let it bother me though. Tomorrow is going to be a long day and since we have no idea what it's going to bring, I want to enjoy this.

Guinevak and Bethany go to a room to change. Even though it's a castle, there aren't many actual bedrooms. They peruse the area, looking to see what each nook and cranny has hiding. It's more elaborate than the house Guinevak lives in, even though she has wood and marble everything, this room is trimmed in gold. The bedposts stand ten feet high or so, covered in deep blue satin, and tied back with golden silk ropes. The fireplace is lined with gold cherubs, and the marble glistens as the flames dance back and forth.

In the corner, is another bed, but this one is a canopy style with a matching blue tapestry to the other one. A sheer curtain lines the circumference of the bed, and the blue satin ties back against the tall bedpost. Bethany grazes her hand over the satin bed cover, giving her goosebumps from how soft it's. She moves slowly to the window where she rests a knee on the chaise lounge placed underneath it. The heel of her shoe clunks on the wooden floor as she places her foot back down.

Meanwhile, Guinevak begins to explore the cabinets of clothes resting on each side of the room. Pulling out a few pieces, she wonders if some of these belonged to Morgana at any point.

Bethany finally checks the other cabinet for something to change into. Guinevak had given her something to change into back at the house, but she doesn't feel comfortable in a dress. Moving things from side to side, she finds a leather jacket with a long train in the back. Moving more, she comes across a shirt lacing up above the bodice. Finally, she opens a drawer and finds a pair of leather riding pants.

Taking it all to the bed, she tries to take the dress off but is having some difficulty. "Can you help me get this thing off?"

In her own little world, she would never have imagined all the fine clothes she is looking at. "In a minute."

"You know, if you are going to do any fighting, a dress is probably not a good idea."

"Yes, but this is dinner, not fighting. Besides, one of those knights could be my husband one day, so I have to look good."

"You are ridiculous."

"Maybe so, but I am smart about it." She pulls a dress from the cabinet and holds it up for Bethany to see. "What do you think?"

"I think a gold merchant mated with a jewel merchant and the dress is their child." Bethany continues to struggle with the dress.

"You are no fun." Guinevak lifts the dress to examine it. In front of her sits an off-white dress embroidered with gold flowers and leaves covering the skirt. The top half is a simple off-white satin with small-embroidered flowers along the top, with diamond centers. The bodice comes down into a 'v' between her breasts and rests off the shoulders. The sleeves are double layered with the long flowing overlay on top of a fitted sleeve covered in the same gold flowers. She knows by the look, it should fit her perfectly.

"Seriously, can you come help me?"

Guinevak lays the dress on the bed and makes her way over. "So how much do you know about this fighting stuff?"

"I've learned a lot from my guardian. I know she probably thinks I still have no idea what I am doing though." She begins to wiggle out of the dress and Guinevak finishes unlacing the back. "What about you?"

"My father taught me some things, but not much. We would practice whenever he got the chance."

"Finish getting dressed. We will practice a little before we go eat."

Guinevak makes her way back to the other bed and tries to remove her own dress. "Your turn." She gives me a pleading look. Throwing the shirt on, Bethany makes her way to Guinevak and begins unlacing the back of her dress.

"Ya know, if you want to learn to fight, Gwen and Luthor can teach you."

"I know. I don't know what I would do with it after this is over."

"At least you will know how to defend yourself."

"True, but then what will I have my knight for."

"Impossible. Your knight won't always be around ya know."

"How do you know?"

"If he is, then he will not be a knight anymore."

"How so?" Guinevak becomes perplexed.

"Think about it. If you marry a knight, do you think he will always come home in the evenings? He is a knight, they fight, go off to war, and do errands for the king."

"I never thought about it."

"Chin up buttercup. How about this, forget the fighting for now. Let's go eat, I am hungry."

"Tie me up first please?" Guinevak struggles to hold the dress up.

"It's not something I ever thought a girl would say to me."

When Guinevak doesn't return the humor, Bethany knows Guinevak has no idea what she is talking about. "Hold on to the bedpost honey, this might hurt a little."

Guinevak grabs the bedpost while Bethany begins to pull strings to tighten the back of the dress.

Guinevak and Bethany finally join us, and I have never seen my sister so regal looking, even though she is wearing pants. They sit at the table and begin grabbing things off of the trays to eat. When she reaches for a pitcher of wine, I slap her hand, and it hits the table with a thump. "I don't think so."

She gives me a pleading look, but I can tell she is not mad. She shakes it off and grabs a pitcher of water instead, filling her goblet while she tears into a piece of chicken leg.

"Eat up, brother. This could be your last meal."

"I find your humor less than adequate sister."

"Girls knock it off, we are here to have a good time." Gwen smacks my arm and gives Bethany a glare.

Once we are done eating, we all gradually disperse to our quarters. When we get to Gwen's room, I pull off some of the layers of clothing I have on. Gwen only has on a shirt and her normal leggings, so she is not as uncomfortable.

"I love this outfit, but man does it not like me."

"Try wearing a corset." She removes her waist cincher.

"So, what do you think will happen tomorrow?"

"No idea to be honest. I think most of it's in Merlin's hands with the potions he has. Capturing them might not be easy though since they still do have magic on their side." Gwen makes her way to me on the other side of the room.

"True. It would be nice if there was someone else that could help hold them back magically so we could get to them easier."

"I wish we did too."

"I have something to ask you, and you can't get mad at me."

"Ok."

"If something happens to me, I want you to be responsible for Bethany. I want you to become her guardian."

Gwen lifts her head and stares forward. She doesn't respond right away, and I can't tell by her expression what she is thinking. "I."

"What?"

"As much as I want to say yes, there are two things. First, it's not my decision. Secondly, I don't want to think about this having to be a thing."

"I know you don't want to think about it, but even if it doesn't happen now, it could on any task we go to."

"I guess you're right. All I can do is petition the guardians and see what happens."

"That's all I can ask then."

Bethany begins to sit with Guinevak and some of the knights after the feast is over. There are still a lot of people in the great hall, and the echo of their voices make it seem much louder.

In a way, she feels sorry for them. They are going up against something they may know nothing about. It breaks her heart to know some of these men may lose their lives tomorrow. As the thoughts continue in the back of her mind, she listens intently to the knight sitting across from me. His name is Lamorak, and he is quite the talker.

"My father is King Pellinore, and my brother is Percival." He points to the other side of the room. "Some say I am one of the strongest Knights of the Round Table. I have been praised as being one of three knights most noted for my deeds of prowess. I began jousting at an early age and received a degree not long after beginning my training. I believe I have excelled ever since. There have been several occasions where I have fought over thirty knights by myself."

Bethany continues to listen, getting bored with the praise of himself. Her attention is drawn to Guinevak's continuous giggling with whoever it's she is talking to. She turns to look at her, and Guinevak gives me a wink.

Looking back at the Lamorak, Bethany decides she is done for the night, and it's time to say goodbye. "Well." she stretches and fake yawns, "I should be getting to bed. It was nice meeting you." Before he can answer, she gets up and makes her way to Guinevak's side.

"Behave."

"What's the fun in that?" Guinevak giggles again, while Bethany heads for the door.

"So, Sir Yvain, tell me more about yourself." Guinevak fawns over him.

Gwen and I decide to go for a walk and find ourselves along one of the paths on top of the castle wall, above the iron gate. Standing there staring at the stars, it's peaceful and quiet. We don't really say anything to each other; it's nice being here.

While we blankly stare into the outskirts of the castle, we are startled by a sudden thud shaking the castle walls. Gwen and I brace ourselves against the stone as a crack of the bricks begins to sound below us. We rise slowly and lean between the cut crevices of the wall to look below us.

There, climbing the wall is the dragon who guarded Bethany in the confines. Gwen reaches for her bow, readying an arrow. I reach for the sword and delight in the sound it makes when I pull it from the sheath. I back up to prepare myself while Gwen stays where she is, steadying herself to pierce its skull with one blow.

Letting off the arrow, it touches its target. Instead of going through the thick scales, it bounces off one of the horns on its head. She backs up towards me, stringing another arrow. We can see the tip of its snout coming over the edge of the wall. Before Gwen can let off another arrow, the dragon rests its head between the square cut out of the wall. The fire from the torches makes its eyes shine, and as I watch it, I can see a sadness you normally would not think from a dragon.

It comes up a few more inches, leaving its body covered by the wall, but its head and neck are exposed. It turns towards Gwen and moves its head three times before finishing its climb. Why is it not attacking us? What does it want?

I can hear footsteps coming from below us, and I know we will be joined shortly by other knights. Before they reach us, the dragon makes its way fully over the wall, and begins inching towards Gwen. Instead of standing and walking towards us, it cowers along the walkway and slithers. Its head is lowered, and its eyes grow sadder, the closer it gets. It stops a foot or so from Gwen and lays there doing nothing.

As the knights come up the stairs, the dragon moves closer, curling itself behind Gwen and pulling a wing forward to cover her legs. If you can imagine a dog resting at your feet, that is what it looks like. Is he friendly? Why is he being like this towards Gwen?

It's startled when the knights bust through the door on both sides. I raise my hand to them as they all draw their weapons. "Lower your weapons."

Gwen stands still and silent through the whole thing. As the dragon stands in protective mode, she begins to hear things around her, the sound of a heartbeat, or the whistle of the wind through a tunnel. She looks around to see if anyone else is hearing it, but they all seem to be paying attention to the dragon.

Suddenly, she hears a deep and raspy voice in her head. Again, she looks around to see if she is hearing things, but she only hears silence and the small sounds she is experiencing.

"Good evening, Guinevere."

"Who are you?"

"Look below you."

She looks down at the dragon and does a double take when it winks at her. *"I have something for you."*

"What? What do you have for me?"

"Information."

"What kind of information?"

"I know what Morgana and Morgause are planning."

"Please tell me."

I look at Gwen and call her name. She raises her hand to hold me off, but I have no idea why. Mouthing the words 'one minute', she closes her eyes and stands perfectly still. I watch as she lowers herself to meet the dragon on its level. I am thoroughly confused by this until I notice her lips moving slightly. *Is she talking to it?*

"They are hiding in a small cavern not far from the confines you freed me from. There you will find them plotting their revenge on the king. From what I know before my release, there will be poison."

"Is that all?"

"That's all I know. Though it's the Lady of the Lake who freed me, I am indebted to you for allowing me to go free."

"But I shot you."

"Yes, but if you would not have come for the girl, I would not be free today. I will do my best to protect you. For now, I must go."

The dragon begins to unwind itself from Gwen's legs and rises from the ground, causing the men to draw again. It turns its head to everyone before standing on the edge of the wall. The flapping of its wings blows us back a bit, and with one final flap, it lifts into the air and begins its flight from the castle.

"What the hell was that all about?" Bethany comes from behind one of the knights.

"I'll tell you inside." She begins to walk towards the door and back into the castle.

We all gather back into the room with the Round Table. I sit in my chair, and she begins to tell us what happened between her and the dragon.

"He spoke to me."

There are a few gasps from the knights and the servants, but not everyone is as shocked.

"Send for Merlin."

"It, he told me where to find Morgana and Morgause. He also told me part of what they are planning."

"What is it?"

"He said they hide in a cave not far from the confines where they had Bethany. He also told me they are planning revenge against Arthur. The only thing he knows is poison will be involved, and he will do his best to protect us."

"So, we know where to find them then." I turn to them all. "Get some rest, we leave at first light. Lancelot, I want you to intercept Merlin and tell him what we know."

"Yes, sire."

Gwen and I go back to her chambers. I want to make sure she is ok before I go to bed myself. She seems shaken by her experience, and I don't want her to go to bed frightened. She is strong, but even the strongest need support occasionally.

"I can't believe this happened." She begins to take off her boots.

I go to her and sit on the chaise beside her. She gets up and moves behind the screen in the corner. I can barely see her shadow as she changes into a nightdress.

"Do you want me to stay?"

"Will you?" She begins to take out her hair.

"Of course. Give me a pillow and a blanket. I'll lie here."

"No, here." She pats the bed.

"Are you sure about that ?"

"Yes. Are you afraid I'll take advantage of you or something?"

"I am afraid for my virtue."

"Oh lord. There is another nightdress in the cabinet. You're not wearing your boots to bed." She crawls in under the covers.

"Fine, be that way. So, what do you think of all this?"

"I think it's a lot of crazy."

"I agree." I make my way to the bed, crawling in on the right side and turn to face her. She is laying on her side facing me with the blanket pulled up, clutching it for dear life. "You have nothing to worry about."

"You are funny, you know?" She taps my nose with the tip of her index finger.

"Funny like haha, or funny looking?" I grab her waist and pull her in close.

"Both."

"Oh, dems fightin words lady." I reach under the covers to find the ticklish spot under her arm.

She laughs profusely, but it only lasts a few seconds when we both stop suddenly. She looks at me flat lipped and confused. I look back into her eyes and say the first thing coming to my mind. "I love you."

"I know."

We kiss as I wrap my arms around her waist again and pull her back in, meanwhile our lips never break free of each other. After a minute or so, she pulls away and turns away from me. She is not hurt or upset this time, and there is a calm about her. I keep my arm around her , holding her tight as we close our eyes and drift off.

Wait, what am I doing here?

Gwen wakes up in one of the last places she expected to be, Olympus. Zeus is standing by the water's edge, and even though he knows she is there, he doesn't acknowledge her. He stares at the glistening water reflecting the rays of the sun until she stands by his side.

"It's about time you come to visit." He chuckles.

"Whose fault is that?"

"Fair." He turns to her. "So, tell me how you are."

He places two large hands on her shoulders and pulls me in a large bear bug.

"I am ok, but I can't breathe."

Zeus slowly releases her. "And what of your new adventures? Did Luthor tell you I visited him?"

"We are in Camelot now, getting ready to fight against two sorceresses, and I don't recall if he did or not."

"Have you considered my offer anymore?"

"What offer?"

"To make you mortal."

"Oh. To be honest, I haven't. I have been so preoccupied with everything else going on, I haven't been able to think about it." Nevertheless, she is thinking about it now.

"You are thinking about it now, aren't you?"

"Of course, I am."

"I will make you the same offer once more. If you wish to have your powers stripped to allow you the life of a mortal human girl, say the word." He turns back to the water.

"Thank you, but right now, I don't think it's something I want."

"Are you sure?" He makes her second-guess herself. When she doesn't reply, he knows the answer. "Wake now, I will come again to you after you have been victorious in your battle."

I open my eyes and realize I am still where I fell asleep, with Gwen wrapped in my arms. She wiggles a little and turns to face me, "Good morning."

"Good morning. How did you sleep?"

"Not bad." She blinks a few times. "I had another dream."

"Tell me about it?"

"It was Zeus. We were standing by the river and he asked me if I wanted him to grant me the ability to be mortal again." She turns away from me.

"What did you say?"

"I told him I am not ready yet. He said the offer still stands and he will visit me again after the battle with Morgana and Morgause."

"You have been having a lot of these dreams. Do you think there is something to them?"

"I have no idea actually. They vary, and it's hard to say. They feel so real, and yet I wake up and it's like nothing happened."

"How many have you had now?"

"Three I think."

"Really?"

"Yeah. First, it was the dream with the two women in the stone confines. That's how I knew where to find Bethany. The second was the snake woman, which I need to speak to Guinevak about. She was in the dream too, and apparently, it was the Queen mother who took Echidna's baby. Then, there is the one from last night with Zeus. I wish I knew what it all meant."

"Maybe it's a new power or another trial."

"Maybe."

Before we can continue our conversation, someone knocks on the door. I can't even get out a 'leave me alone' or 'come in' before the door opens.

Bethany opens the door slowly and peaks her head in. Guinevak leans in behind her. I hide under the covers, not wanting them to see me. When Bethany and Guinevak open the door further, Gwen speaks up, "I am not decent. Let me get dressed first and I will meet you outside the great hall."

"Ok." Both girls turn and close the door behind them.

Giving it a moment, I slowly slide back up to the pillows. I look at Gwen and her nerves subside. She does her best to hide her laughter, but she can't control it. I pull her down to me and wrap her in my arms again. I give her an Eskimo kiss with my nose, and she returns the gesture with a real one.

"We gotta go."

"Ugh, do we have to?"

"Seriously, Luthor, the fake whine?"

" I can't help it."

"Get up, and get dressed, dork."

Both of us retreat from the bed. I let her go first to change, and as she comes out to put on her boots, I go behind the wall.

When we are both finished, I look at her with a slight smirk. "Maybe we should leave separately.

"Good idea. Wait like twenty seconds after me, then go."

"Yes, ma'am."

Gwen leaves first and meets Bethany and Guinevak outside the great hall. Not to make things obvious, I wait a few minutes before following behind. They are still standing there when I come down the grand staircase to meet them. The three girls look at me, and I can tell by their mischievous expressions they know.

"How did you sleep brother?" Bethany glances at Gwen.

"Just fine, thank you. Shall we eat?"

"We shall." Guinevak leads us in.

The doors to the great hall are already open, and most of the people are seated and eating. Like dinner, the candelabras are lit, and the food is spread across the table. Toast, eggs, large sausages, wine, you name it; it covered every inch of the tables. I take my place in the same spot as last night and fill my plate. There are small wooden spoons in mugs every so often on the table. Apparently, they don't want us to eat eggs with our fingers.

"Gentleman, ladies, if you are finished, I believe it's time to convene to the round table."

"Yes, sire."

"Luthor, Lancelot, Luthor."

"Yes, sire."

"Oh, for the love, just go."

It's time to go over our plans again, one last time before heading out. "Is everyone clear on what they are doing?"

They respond as some give a 'yes, sire' as well. I know Bethany will need to review some tactics before I allow her to fight anything. Before I speak to her, the doors open and Angelic walks through. The sound of wood scraping marble echoes as the men stand to greet her.

"Angelic?"

"Good morning, Luthor."

"How did you get here?" I make my way toward her.

"They brought me last night." She points to Tristan and Gawain.

"Why are you here?"

"I am here to help."

She moves to a seat not far from Gwen. Giving Bethany and Gwen acknowledgement, she takes her place to wait and see what the plan is.

We all follow her lead and take our seats. I begin by reiterating what is happening for Angelic. "So here is what will be happening. Before we go anywhere, a few of our fighters need to have more practice. Now, since Angelic is here, she can take Bethany to spar and make sure she is ready. Guinevak will need to be prepared as well." I pause and look at Lady Ragnall. "I would like you to combine forces with Angelic and take Guinevak and Bethany to practice."

"Yes, sire"

"I give up." I whisper to myself as I place my face in my hands.

I get a look from Bethany as she begins to leave the room. I know she is upset with me since I am making her train, but I shrug it off. I know what I am doing is right, and she will see soon too.

"Men, I want you to go to the armory. Take what you feel will be needed and meet me inside the front gate in one hour."

"Yes, sire." Lancelot adds. "What about you and her majesty?"

"Why do you keep calling me that?"

"Calling you what?"

"Your majesty, why do you keep calling me that?" She approaches him.

"As a sign of respect, my lady. You are after all the queen to be."

Gwen turns towards me, and I can see the shock in her face. She mouthed '*what*' to me before turning back to Lancelot. "I see. Well then, I shall see you on the battlefield."

Lancelot looks to me for direction, and I shrug. He leaves and takes the men with him. I am then left with a shocked and confused Gwen.

"Come here." I move towards her.

She is hesitant but lets me hold her for a moment. "I am worried."

"About what?"

"All of this. We battled magic before with Hera, but this time seems different. There are two of them now." She pulls away to look me in the eye.

"You aren't still thinking about the end of the story, are you?"

"Shouldn't I?" She pulls away completely and turns her back towards me.

"I can't die, if I do, how will you become queen?" I bow behind her.

She turns and hits me on the head, and I stay in my bow. "You aren't funny."

"I think I am." I rub the spot she hit and stand.

"Come on, we need to get ready." She turns away and heads for the door.

We all meet outside in the courtyard where Guinevak and Bethany are in full force, sparring with Angelic and Lady

Ragnall. Iron hitting iron echoes through the courtyard like a battlefield of a hundred men.

"Ladies and gentlemen." The quartet of women stop fighting long enough to catch their breath and hear what I have to say.

I look around at the fifty plus people standing before me. It's more than I expected there to be. I look to my left and can see three grooms bringing horses towards us. "Your horses, sire."

"Thank you. As I was saying, it's now or never. I hope you are all ready to face these two treasonous women. Keep your heads high and your wits about you. They are not to be trusted, and they may have many tricks up their sleeves. Be careful, be alert, and be vigilant. Now, mount up and let's go."

As we mount our horses, and others make formation for those walking, a loud thunder can be heard in the distance. One by one we look up as darkness begins to overshadow us. I smile slightly as the dragon begins to lower itself on the edge of the courtyard wall. Many of the knights draw their swords, but I motion for them to be put away. Reluctantly, they do, but still keep a vigilant eye on it.

"He is here to help us. Be kind and it will be kind to you." I yell out to ease their clear discomfort of the dragon's presence.

I look back up to the dragon, and it stares in acknowledgement.

I turn to say something to Gwen when I realize her face has turned pale, and she seems motionless. I pull on the reins to bring my horse closer to her. Reaching for her, she is warm, but unresponsive. Is she in a trance? What is happening? "Merlin, now!"

"Good morning, your majesty.".

"How is this possible?"

"All is possible with magic."

"How can you speak to me and only me?"

"This is how I am created. I can choose who I speak to."

"And you chose me? Why?"

"I trust you."

"Who created you?"

There is a pause before he answers, *"Morgause."*

"What is it you want?"

"I wanted to thank you once again for freeing me, and to make sure you know I will be following you to find them."

Above us, the dragon shifts slightly, making a bit of the castle wall crumble below him.

"We welcome your help, but we must go."

Gwen suddenly snaps out of it, and notices how close I am. She glances at me, looks up at the dragon, then turns back to me and speaks, "He is coming with us."

"Did he speak to you again?"

"Yes."

"What did he say?"

Then, Merlin joins us. "Are you ready, sire?"

"Men, ladies, are we ready?"

I hear an array of shouts and cheers coming from the knights and the people standing and riding. "Sire." someone calls out, "what about the servants?"

"They know what to do now, so let's go."

We ride towards the confines. It will be a short ride, but I want to make sure everyone is up to par so I decide to go back and forth between everyone on the way there.

As we make it to the confines in less than a half hours' time, we separate in half, each going to one side of the confines and spread out to look for the cave.

About halfway through the search, we dismount our horses and finish the search from on foot. Tying our horses to the trees, we pray nothing will set them free. Who knows what they have lurking in the shadows. The wooded area surrounding the confines is thick with trees and bushes. There are no real paths to follow, so we make our way through the lightest areas we can find.

It's not long before we hear a commotion coming from a few feet away. I look at everyone, signaling quietly to move closer. Before we can get five feet or so to where the sound is coming from, a ball of fire comes out of nowhere, hitting one of the knights in the chest. He flies a few feet backwards, and lands against a large rock. Gwen runs to him, checking his pulse to see if he is breathing. She turns to me and I see by the devastated look in her eyes; he is dead.

"Break their line of sight!" Merlin calls out, and we all move to the sides.

A thin layer of fog rises quickly from the ground below us. It swirls in different patterns and at different points, expanding slowly as it drifts toward the others. Merlin quickly calls to the wind, brushing it away. As he moves his arms, it swirls more, but never stops its advance. Suddenly, it rises, causing us to be visually impaired, enveloping us in pure white. I cough as I move my hand in front of my face to fan it away from me. I can hear the others around me doing the same.

A laughter grows through the dense fog. "I have the power now."

My eyes grow heavy, and I fight to keep my attention on the sound of the women walking towards me. Whatever is in the fog is causing me to become tired and disoriented. It's then I remember Balderon. I know he can help clear the fog, so I do my best to reach him.

"Balderon!" I shout in a weak voice, praying he can hear me.

The rapid flap of his wings cause the fog to stir and move. Within moments, it slowly lowers itself to ground level again. As I look up, Morgause is standing before me. I scramble for my sword as she moves towards me, the low-lying fog twisting and turning at her feet. Her face is contorted with fury, and as she glares at me, she quickly releases her next attack. Suddenly, I am knocked to the ground. Not by a spell, but by another knight. A ball of blue flame hits him in the abdomen, and he goes flying. I start to rise but am slammed back to the ground. I turn my head toward Morgause when I see a thin line of red vapor twisting its way into my chest. I place my hand in the way to block it but all it does is cause my hand to go numb.

I try to reach for my sword, but I have no feeling in my hand to grasp it. I hear Morgause murmur words and it fills me with a slight fear. Is this really how it will end? Is Gwen right? Without hesitation, Merlin steps in front of me and draws a wall of fire to hide us, causing Morgause to stumble backwards.

"Nice try." Merlin holds out his hand.

I can see over the wall of fire as Morgause regains her ground and recomposes herself. She begins to laugh slightly as she too moves her hand, this time vanquishing the fire. "Do you think it's going to be easy old man?"

"No, but this is." He trails off, and I can see Gwen sneaking up behind her.

Grabbing her by the hair, Gwen yanks her head back causing her to scream out in pain. With her mouth open, Gwen pours the binding potion down Morgause's throat, holding her mouth shut, forcing her to swallow. When she lets go of her hair, Morgause falls to her knees, choking.

"What have you done to me?"

While we are concentrating on Morgause, the others are doing their best to fight off Morgana. The men are dodging ball after ball of fire. I can see Angelic and Bethany trying to move in behind her.

With Morgause down for now, Merlin makes his way to them and stands in front of the men.

"Get back."

With a whip of his arms, sparks fly, and puffs of golden fill the area around him and Morgana.

"Now!"

I can hear another yelp, and then a thump. As the fog clears, Morgana is on her knees as well. Before I know what hit me, I am knocked forward. As I hit the ground, I roll to find Morgause over me bearing a large sword. During the first blow, I concentrate on my defense and let my muscles settle into the rhythm of swordplay. She is matching me move for move, and I am tiring.

I can see others out of the corner of my eye moving towards us while others are trying to settle Morgana. I know it will only be moments before they will be captured, and we will take them back to the dungeons.

After several attempts to get past Morgause's defenses, I lose my temper and batter at her to pound her into the ground. I think she expected to defeat me quickly, but she underestimated my anger level. As I force her to the ground-pushing sword on sword, I can see the loss in her face. I back off as a few of the knights disarm her and tie her hands together.

"How?

"What, defeat you?"

Before she can answer, Merlin and Angelic come towards us, having Morgana tied up as well. As she wiggles to free herself, it only makes the restraints tighter.

"You won't get away with this." She breathes out in pure fury.

"Take them away. Put them in the dungeons, separately. Take ten men with you to guard them and take Merlin as well."

As they leave with Morgana and Morgause, I look at my surroundings and realize how many men are lying helpless on the ground.

"We need to help them." Gwen pleads as she comes towards me.

"We need to get them back to the castle. Isn't there some kind of hospital type thing or something?"

"I am sure there is a physician. I know Merlin can help."

"How do we get them back? We can't carry them." I look around, seeing quite a few extra horses. "Men help me get them on the horses."

Once we get the wounded on a horse, we go back for the final three. Their lifeless bodies lay against the rocks and trees. Their chests are still smoldering where the fire hit them. Sadly, I don't even know their names. Instead of putting them on horses, we make a makeshift carriage out of some of the items we find near the cave.

Morgana and Morgause have a small two-wheel cart full of miscellaneous items. We throw them to the ground and gently place the men's bodies on it. Using an old piece of horse blanket, we cover them, tying the cart to the horse using some rope, making sure it will not choke as we ride.

The more we do, the more my heart breaks for them. They died for me and I don't even know their names. What kind of person am I? It's at this moment I decide I will take the reins of what they think I am instead of who I am now. "We must go." I add somberly.

Some of us mount, and others walk with the wounded and the cart.

It takes a lot longer to get back to the castle than it did to get to the confines. We make it through the gate, and those who left before us are already there and getting the horses back to their stables.

Morgana and Morgause are placed in the dungeons on opposite sides, and we dismount the wounded first. They are placed on carts and then wheeled to another part of the grounds where Merlin will tend to their wounds. There are ten, so it takes some time to get them all a place to lie down.

I leave the wounded in Merlin's capable hands, but before I leave him, he makes a comment to me making me second-guess whether or not this was all worth it. "I have twenty-four hours."

"Twenty-four hours for what?"

"To make the binding permanent."

"I thought it was permanent."

"I wish it was." He goes back to tending to the men, and I leave to tend to the deceased.

I make it back to the courtyard, and the bodies of the three men have already been removed from the cart. They are taken to the holding area where they will be prepped by women and then set on a funeral pyre. Gwen stands watch, and everyone else makes their way to their quarters for now.

"Do you think we did the right thing?" I wrap my arm around her waist.

"You mean go after them? Of course, we did the right thing. Why would you ask?" She turns to face me.

"I knew there was a chance people would get hurt, but I didn't think I would feel like it was all for nothing."

"I am not following."

"Merlin told me the potion we used on them is not permanent, so their powers can come back."

"Did he say how long it lasts?"

"Around twenty-four hours."

"Then we have twenty-four hours to make sure this stays permanent. Is he working on the wounded?"

"Yes."

"Good, then let's freshen up, get something to eat, and get a good night's sleep."

"Who were they?" I pause before following her direction. "The ones who died, who were they?"

"I was not sure, so I asked around. Sir Breunor, Sir Galahad, and Sir Morien."

"Who were they as men? Were they good men? I need to know all I can so I can pay them proper tribute." I become frantic at the thought of confronting the men about it.

"Why don't you call the men to the table and let them have their own tribute."

"It's not a bad idea."

We both turn to walk towards the castle. As I approach knights along the way, I make mention to them of everyone meeting at the table in thirty minutes.

Once we are all together, I take my place at the table. I look up at the knights, looking weary, tired, and broken. Those who have minor injuries join us, but the others stay behind.

"I want to raise a glass, not only to you, but to those we lost today. Sir Breunor, Sir Galahad, and Sir Morien were brave in the face of torment, and though they went out fighting, they will always have a place as a Knight of the Round Table."

The men pound their fists on the table and stomp their feet on the floor in cheers.

"I open the floor to anyone who would like to say anything."

Lancelot rises from his chair and begins to speak. "Sir Galahad was a simple soldier. Though he was not as well known among us, he will not be forgotten. Galahad will forever be known to everyone as an exemplar of greatness." As he sits, they pound and stomp again. Cheers of *'here, here,'* and *'huzzah'* are followed.

Gwen steps up next and speaks of Sir Breunor. "Granted his knighthood after saving me from a lion, I can't be more honored to have fought with Sir Breunor. His bravery and loyalty will not be forgotten." Gwen's words are then followed by more stomping and cheers.

Lancelot steps up again to finish the third honor. "If it was not for his father's quest to find me, Morien would not be here today; his mother a princess, his father a knight. He grew into a tall, handsome youth. Of his prowess, Sir Morien's blows are mighty."

As Lancelot sits, the final pounds and stomping commence. I wait a few moments for it to calm down before I speak again. "Tonight, we feast in honor of them.

We then rest, for tomorrow we honor them one last time with the funeral pyre."

Everyone begins to rise from their seats and make their way to the great hall. I stop Gwen before she leaves. "How did you know about him?"

"I don't know, it kind of came to me."

Sitting in her bed, Gwen tries to shake this feeling there should be more to what is going on. Without hesitation, she gets up and makes her way towards Angelic's room a few doors down.

With a gentle knock, she pushes the door open and calls out for Angelic. There is no answer, so she pushes her way in completely, towards the bed, realizing it's empty. Off in the distance, she can hear the clashing of metal. Turning to make her way to the window she sees where the noise is coming from. Peering out, Angelic and Bethany are practicing in the lamp light. "Hey!" she calls down to them. Catching Angelic off guard, Bethany gets a dig into her side. It doesn't cause any damage to her, but it does give her a bit of a shock.

Angelic turns to Bethany and smiles. "Nice."

"Hello up there!" Bethany calls to Gwen.

"Hello down there! Can't sleep?"

Bethany shakes her head, and I look to Angelic for the same response. "Would you like to join us?"

"I'll be down in a second."

Stopping by her room to change and grab a weapon, Gwen makes sure to be quiet.

Once outside, she meets up with Bethany and Angelic. Taking a three-way position, they ready themselves for confrontation.

"So why can't you sleep?" Gwen takes the first shot, advancing towards Bethany.

"No idea. Why can't you?"

"Too much on my mind I suppose."

"Anything you want to talk about?" Angelic blocks the attack.

"I'm not sure." I spin, hitting both of their swords.

"Try me." Angelic advances with a blow to Bethany's leg.

Bethany ducks in time for the blade to make a small rip in her pants. "Oh man, I really liked these."

Instead of pouting about it, Bethany takes it as a sign of war and attacks vigorously at Angelic. "Oh, you want to play little girl?"

Gwen stands back and watches as the two go back and forth. Every once in a while, Bethany will get a point in, but Angelic is holding her own pretty well against her. The question is, is Angelic holding back?

She decides she can't hold it in any longer and blurts out something, making both the women stop and drop their swords. "Luthor is in my room right now sleeping."

"Wait, what?" Bethany gets closer to me.

By her expression, Gwen can't tell if Bethany is happy or mad. "Luthor is in my room sleeping."

"Oh, I heard you the first time." Bethany's voice begins to soften, and her eyes glow with happiness. "It's about damn time."

"Watch your mouth, young lady." Angelic moves and faces Gwen with curiosity and concern. "Is this wise?"

"Nothing has happened yet. There has only been the occasional kiss and maybe some cuddling."

Bethany is still beaming, but Angelic is not having any of it. "What is happening between the two of you?"

"I'm not sure."

"They are in love. They always have been, they just keep fighting it."

"She doesn't know, does she?" Angelic turns to Bethany.

"Know what?"

Gwen turns to her, looking her in the eyes when she tells Bethany the truth. "I can't love."

"What do you mean?"

"She is not allowed to as a Guardian, at least not with someone who is not a Guardian."

"I'm so confused."

"A Guardian can only love and reproduce with another Guardian. It's part of their powers. If they fall in love with a human, whether he be traveler or not, the love they have can literally kill them."

"So, you mean to tell me if you and my brother ever do the thing, it can kill him?"

"Yeah, but there is more."

"There is?" Bethany and Angelic say in unison.

"I was granted the opportunity by Zeus to have my powers stripped as a Guardian and become human so I can love whoever I wanted without consequence."

"Why am I hearing about this now?"

"I was thinking the same thing." Angelic adds.

"It's something I need to think about. I don't want to involve anyone else until I make a final decision."

"And have you?" Bethany moves closer.

"No."

"You know what this means, right?"

"I know. It means I lose everything about who I am."

"It also means your Guardian bloodline dies with you."

"I know."

"Have you made up your mind?" Bethany moves behind me and wraps me up in her arms. "Honestly, it doesn't matter. You have been my sister since the day we met."

Gwen turns in Bethany's arms and squeezes her as hard as she can. "No, I haven't decided. The outcome here is going to be what makes up her mind."

"And what of your trials?" Angelic breaks up the moment.

"What about them? I've only had one." Gwen breaks apart from Bethany and they both face Angelic.

"Are you sure?" Angelic makes her second guess herself.

"Well, there was Camelot."

"And? Think about it. Have you experienced anything since Camelot?"

Bethany doesn't say anything, but watches Gwen's face change from thought to understanding. "The dreams?"

"What dreams?"

"I have been having these dreams that seem so real. The first one is when I found the women at the confines. The second is like a continuation of an old dream, and the third is Zeus pulling me back to Olympus to ask me about his offer."

"And you say they feel real?"

"Yeah."

"Do you experience anything after you wake?"

"After the second dream, my arm hurt where Echidna had scratched me." She reaches up and rubs the spot on her arm.

"How long have you been having dreams like this?" Bethany cuts us off.

"While in Olympus, your brother and I had similar dreams more than once, but now I am having them on my own."

"Well, I do believe these are the second set of trials. Consult the book and see what it says." Angelic instructs. "Let's call it a night, it's getting late."

I'm not wearing that...

Gwen's worry makes me think every time I write in this journal will be the last time ever. Circumstances what they are, I proved her wrong, and I'm still here.

As much as I love doing this, I look forward to going home and relaxing. A part of me wants to call this home as well though, because I like it here. Oh sure, I liked it on Olympus too, but I can't go back there and call it home. Here, I can become who they think I am; I can be the king. Who wouldn't want that? There is only one thing to change my mind and she is lying right next to me. She still has a decision to make and if she decides to not go through with Zeus's offer, then I will have no choice but to go home with her instead of having her stay here with me, as the queen.

I have dreamed of the day, I honor my promise and not force her to make the choice, and I won't try to sway her *either way. I care for her too much to have her miserable with whatever she chooses.*

Now, let's talk about my sister. Good God can she stop growing up now? She has come so far from when we first started this adventure, and even though she has a tendency to do the teenage girl, whiny, rebellious thing, she still has become so much more. I know for a fact it has nothing to do with me, because God knows I am no help. I will definitely let Angelic and Gwen take all the credit for this one. If I do decide to stay here, she will always have a place with me too, but I won't force her to stay if she doesn't want to.

These knights have gone through so much for me already, and I have no idea how to repay them for their kindness. Gwen tells me Tristan has given her a clue the mission is really more for my benefit than theirs. He never did explain how, but I think now I know what my true spirit is.

We only have a few hours left until the powers are fully restored to Morgana and Morgause. I hope Merlin is working some kind of magic to find a more permanent solution.

I am already awake when Gwen turns to me and smiles. I can tell by her face she is still tired. How much sleep has she really gotten? I know at some point I woke up on the chaise and she was not there. I fell back to sleep in the bed, and she still was not back yet.

"You're staring again."

"I can't help it." I lean in and kiss her forehead.

"So now we have stopped two evil sorceresses, what do we do now?" She raises herself to a sitting position. "Disney World?"

"We say goodbye to three good knights." I get up and make my way to a chair on the other side of the room. I grab my knickers and boots and move back towards the bed. Kissing her again on the forehead, I say my goodbye. "I am going to go take a bath and change my clothes."

"Ok."

I turn away before she catches my arm. "Um, before I forget, don't be mad, ok?"

"About what?"

"They know."

Gwen leaves it there and I head for my chambers.

Gwen goes to the door, and a servant enters with a bucket of hot water. Bowing, she makes her way to the bathtub and begins adding the water to what is already there. She places the bucket down, grabs another one from near the fire, and adds it as well. Running her fingers through, she bows again before leaving.

"Is there anything you require before I go, my lady?"

"No, thank you."

"I will go then."

Gwen disrobes as she makes her way to the bathtub. Stepping in, a warmth runs through her body, starting at her toes and making its way to her head. She can see the goosebumps forming on her skin, and it makes her giggle slightly. She slowly sinks in and lets the heat take over.

She must have fallen asleep at some point, because the servant opening the door awakens her. Shocked at seeing her in the tub still, the servant jumps back, covers her eyes, and excuses herself while apologizing profusely.

Gwen laughs it off and raises herself from the tub. As she grabs the robe hanging there, she strokes the sleeves. "Like a baby bunny, so soft."

She lets herself dry as she makes her way to the dressing table. Sitting down in front of the distorted mirror, she brushes her hair. Then, a knock on the door startles her again.

Guinevak peaks in, catching sight of me. "Oh, sister bonding time?"

"Sure." Gwen reaches out the brush to Guinevak.

"How did you sleep?"

"Like crap."

"Sister!"

"Sorry, I am not used to this whole proper woman thing."

"I am sure it will take time. So, what are we dressing in today?"

"Well, I am guessing since it's a funeral, and I am the queen to be, I should dress appropriately."

Guinevak stops brushing for a minute and takes in what Gwen has just said. Turning to face her, Gwen sees the tears Guinevak is trying to hide. "What?"

"You admitted what you are."

"Oh, stop it and brush her hair."

Guinevak grabs a few pins off the table and begins to work her magic. As she places it up in a new style, she continues with more questions. "So, does this mean you are thinking about staying?"

"It means I will do my duty while I am here, and we will see what happens."

"What about Arthur?"

"What about him?"

"Well, you are betrothed to him, aren't you?"

"No, Guinevere is betrothed to Arthur. I am betrothed to no one."

"So, you are going to pretend?"

"Are you finished? I have to get dressed." Gwen rises from the chair. Guinevak's questions are ruining her perfectly calm morning.

"What did I say?"

"There are things I will admit, and one is in this life, here in Camelot, I am your sister. I as in Guinevere, not I as Gwen. Another thing I will admit to is I, here in Camelot am betrothed to King Arthur. I as in Guinevere, not I as Gwen. You need to understand the difference. Until I decide on which one I want to be permanently, I am both. So, in here, I am Gwen talking to Guinevak. When I walk out there, I will be Guinevere, betrothed to King Arthur, standing by his side while he says goodbye to the brave knights." After her rant, she makes her way to one of the closets.

"Wow."

"Wow? Really, that's all you have to say?"

"I can honestly say I have nothing else to add. You have made it clear how you feel about it."

"Don't you dare act like I am a horrible person for not taking on the side of me you want me to be."

"Maybe I should go."

"Probably a good idea."

By now, I am back to my room, and the first thing I do is strip down and make my way to the bathtub, the water feeling so good on my skin. You would think by the relaxing noises I make, I haven't ever taken one before, but the enjoyment doesn't last long. I am probably in there for about twenty minutes when a servant comes in to check on me.

"Sire, I have been asked to inform you that the funeral pyres are ready." He bows out the door.

"I guess this means I get to go play king now."

I find a towel laying on a small stool not far from the bath. Wrapping myself up, I dry off as I search for what to wear. I know my normal traveler's clothes aren't going to cut it, so I search the closets. I wonder if kings wear black or not for these kinds of things.

In one of the cabinets, I find a loose set of armor. I pull each piece out, not understanding how to put any of it on, so I lay each piece on the bed and proceed to get dressed in the peasant shirt and knickers. They are like the ones I wear as a traveler, but black. There is a chainmail looking shirt with a hood, so I put it on next.

There is another knock at the door, and it opens slowly. A curly head peaks in, and I call for Tristan to come in. As he enters, he sees me struggling to finish getting ready. "Let me help you."

Over the chain mail shirt, we put another layer of a red sleeveless tunic with a golden dragon on the front. On top is a one-shoulder piece of armor going around my neck. A brown belt holds the middle together, and then a set of black leather gloves covers my hands.

"There is something missing."

"My boots, I am not sure how I am going to get those on."

"No, sire, the cape and the crown."

"I am not wearing the crown."

"Then the cape." He searches through some of the cabinets and closets to find it. Meanwhile, I know he has come in for a reason.

"Is there something you wanted?"

"Just to make sure you were ready."

I catch something red and stop him. "Is this it?"

"No, sire. Ah, here it's."

He pulls out a long jet-black cape almost longer than he is tall. He brings it to me and places it on my shoulders. Coming to the front, he clasps it together with two large, black coin-like hooks.

"Is there something on this too?" I try to look behind me.

"What do you mean?"

"An insignia, like the dragon."

"Yes, the same one, but larger."

"I see."

"We should get going."

"After you." I motion for him to head off as I follow behind. Now I know why they move so slow in the movies, this stuff weighs a ton.

Bethany and Angelic are already there waiting in the courtyard, as are Lady Ragnall and Guinevak. I can't tell why, but there is definite tension between Guinevak and Gwen.

I move closer, and notice Bethany, Guinevak, and Angelic are definitely not dressed for the occasion. Angelic and Guinevak bow, and Bethany approaches me with determination in her eyes.

"Once this is over, there is something that needs fixing."

"Gwen and Guinevak?"

"How did you guess?"

"You can cut the tension with a knife."

As I make my way towards the funeral pyres, everyone else begins to follow behind me. I look over to Gwen who has made her way to my side, and almost can't breathe at how amazingly gorgeous she looks in black.

Her outfit shapes her perfectly, as it was meant for her. The bodice cuts above her breasts, and the silver along the front shimmers in the sunlight. The pattern running down the front of the dress is not familiar to me, but it resembles a basic swirl with the occasional leaf motif. The edges of the material are trimmed with a silver and black ribbon, encrusted with what I would assume are black pearls, and the neckline is trimmed in black lace.

The sleeves of the dress flare out at the end, and the same material on the front trims the center and the cuff. The jet-black velvet matches my cape, and she is wearing a silver belt clasping in the front, hanging all the way to her feet. The jewelry around her neck is covered in black pearls and sits inside silver settings.

As we come up on the funeral pyre, instead of having three separates, they made one large one. The three knights are already on top, and their swords have been placed on the ground in front of the pyre with the helmets resting on top. I turn to face everyone and brace myself to make one of the most important speeches I feel I will ever have to make in my life.

"This is a moment no one ever wants to endure. Today we say goodbye to three of the bravest men we know. They died fighting for something they believed in, and on this day, we let their lives light the sky above us. For now, they are our light, and they will guide us from here on out. Let light be your beacon of hope and know when tomorrow comes, you will always have your brothers in arms standing beside you in life, in death, and forever. Today we celebrate not only their lives, but our own. We celebrate our victory over tyranny and hardship, over struggle and pain. Today we celebrate the right to live."

The cheers die down as a servant brings out four torches. He hands one to me, one to Gawain, one to Lancelot, and one to Tristan. We each take a side of the pyre and place the torches in different spots. When it's lit enough, we back up and throw the torches into the flames.

Joining the rest, we watch as the fires grow, and it reminds me of watching my own mother. The pain takes everything I have not to pull out the pocket watch and open it. I look over at Bethany, and there are tears streaming down her face. Is she thinking the same thing?

Without hesitation, Angelic moves in behind her and places an arm around her shoulder. She is her protector, her guardian, her calm. I watch as Bethany instantly begins to relax, and I know no matter what happens to me, Bethany will always be ok as long as Angelic is there to guide her.

The mourning is interrupted, and as I turn to see what the commotion is, I can blindly see a figure coming from the castle. Dirty, ragged, and torn, the woman's hair has clearly been disheveled by the torment of being cooped up. Her screams are ear piercing, and as she runs towards us.

Morgana edges closer, and the knights scramble from behind the pyre to catch her. She has her arms stretched out, and I know she is trying her best to produce some kind of magic. A few random sparks fly from her fingertips, but nothing really happens, meaning her magic hasn't come back yet.

The first few knights catch up with her and are able to subdue her arms first. She begins to spit off words in Latin as I make my way closer to where the knights are holding her. I call for a few to come and take Gwen and the others away from the scene.

They don't make it far before she breaks free of their grasp and heads towards me again. They grab her, and this time hold her down on the ground instead of on her feet. As they are about to tie her hands together, I catch sight of Merlin making his way towards her carrying a vile in his hand.

"Hold her still."

Morgana does her best to wiggle and thrash to break free as he pours another concoction down her throat. Within seconds, she stops moving long enough for the knights to tie her arms and legs together like a pig. As he makes his way to me, carrying a second vile, I look to the knights again and ask them to escort Gwen, Angelic, Bethany, Guinevak and Lady Ragnall away from the pyres.

Merlin's face changes expression from triumph to fear as he speeds up his pace in my direction. By now, the women are far enough away they don't see what is coming next. As Merlin calls out for me to turn around, I feel a sharp sting near my inner thigh. Almost collapsing, I turn, coming face to face with Morgause. How did she escape? How did they both escape?

Growing weaker, I try my best to stand and reach for my sword. Happy with herself, Morgause backs away slowly, staring at the blade. She whispers something too quiet to hear and then draws the blade across her palm. Dropping it to the ground, she rubs her hands together as she continually repeats a chant. Other than the normal weakness, I feel nothing changing around me.

In the background, I can hear Gwen and Bethany screaming. I keep telling myself I have to stay awake, and I have to fight. I gather what strength I have, and I charge towards her, leaving a trail of blood behind me.

She is quick enough, as she picks up the dagger and blocks my first attack. I withdraw the sword and swing at her again. Between the weight of the armor and the weakness I am experiencing, there is no way I will win. I decide to back away as quickly as I can, unclasping the cape with one hand and letting it drop to the ground. Next, comes the shoulder armor as she advances towards me and tries to strike again. This time I block her advance and use my leg to kick her back.

She stumbles far enough away it gives me a chance to rip off the piece of armor. She comes at me again, and this time her dagger connects the chain mail, but never makes it through. I elbow her in the jaw, and she falls to the ground. I need to get the rest of this off, and quickly.

I tear at the red tunic and it comes off easy enough. With the chain mail shirt on now, I advanced towards her, but as I am about to reach her, my leg gives out. I fall to the ground only a few feet away, and I can hear her laugh. I look up and she is wiping blood off her face as she slowly paces towards me.

I roll to my stomach, and look up to see a few of the knights holding back the women. The women, three of the most important things in my life. I need to finish this for them, but before I can get to my feet, I feel another sharp sting to my other leg and I holler in pain.

I can hear footsteps running towards me, and I know some of the knights are coming to assist me. "No! This is my fight and my fight alone."

As Morgause is about to take another stab at me, I turn in time to feel my sword plunge into her chest. A look of shock and horror grows on her face, and I know she feels the defeat. I don't realize she has contacted me as well. As my adrenaline dies, I feel the pain in my side growing. Dropping, I reach for the open area around my armpit where there is no chain mail. Pulling the hand away, I watch as blood runs down my fingers.

Morgause is lying at my feet, and I know this is over for her and Morgana. The problem with it all is I feel it's over for me too. I grow weaker and lose my ability to stand anymore. The weight of the sword makes me drop it to the ground, and as my head hits the grass, the sound of Gwen's voice fades to silence.

Bethany and Gwen do their best to free themselves from the knight's grasp. They can barely see what is happening between the flames and the tears filling their eyes.

Once the knights let them go, they run with everything they have left in us. There is blood soaking the surrounding ground. Behind them, Morgause is trying her best to get to her feet.

As Gwen screams for help, Lancelot and Tristan restrain Morgause. Knowing she is too injured to fight back, she doesn't resist them. Merlin approaches first and tries to push Bethany out of the way, but she will not move. "I need to get to him."

Reluctantly, she moves so Merlin can kneel, pulling out another vile from his belt. He begins to chant as he waves his hand. "The rest is up to him now." Merlin stands and makes his way to Morgause.

Before he can get close enough, she spits at him and laughs with what little energy she has left. He grabs her by the jaw and she begins to wiggle from his grasp. Forcing her mouth open, he pours a liquid in as he quietly whispers the incantation. "Take her away."

Morgause only makes it a few feet before her face goes completely white and she collapses out of Lancelot and Tristan's arms. "Bring her, because I have a special place for her and Morgana."

Once they are all back inside, Merlin leaves with Morgana and Morgause in the dungeons to finish his task while the rest of them take Luthor to his chambers. They place him on the left side of the bed, and the knights fetch for the local apothecary to bring a poultice and some bandages. He is still unresponsive, but he is breathing.

Everyone else is shooed away from the room other than Bethany and Gwen. As they stand watch, the apothecary undresses him and tends to his wounds. The poultice she uses smells horrible, and you would hope that alone will at least wake him, but it doesn't. The girls sit, holding each other on the chaise under the window while the apothecary does her thing.

Once she is finished, she leaves a bowl of water and a towel next to the bed. "He needs to stay cool in order for his fever to come down.; use the towel and water. Keep an eye on him to watch when his fever breaks."

"What about the wounds?"

"The poultice will stop the bleeding, Bethany, but it will take some time. These are very dangerous wounds, and she came very close to his heart. He has lost a lot of blood. The rest is up to him now."

"Two people have said it now."

"He knows he has a lot to live for. He won't give up easily."

Gwen moves to Luthor's bedside and pats his forehead with the cloth as instructed. He is sweating profusely, and there seems to be no end in sight. She worries, and if Bethany paces any more, there will be a hole in the floor.

"How long has it been?"

"I don't know, Bethany. My cell phone doesn't work here, so there is no way to see the time."

Bethany looks out the window and does her best to judge by where the sun is in the sky. "I know it has been at least a day. Shouldn't it have at least subsided by now?"

"It's hard to say." Merlin's voice breaks the frustration as he enters the room. "His body suffered three major blows. This can take some time to recover from."

"If his fever breaks, it's a good sign, right? Is there anything else you can do?"

Gwen pleads with Merlin for any positive answer.

"The potion I gave him yesterday should have stimulated the healing process. If it's not working by now, there may have been something on the blade Morgause stabbed him with that is counteracting it."

"So, he could still die. No, I won't allow it. They have too much to accomplish together. Do you hear me, Lu? You need to wake up. You need to fight."

"Gwen." Bethany grabs her and pulls her in. "He will pull through this. We have to be patient. I know my brother, he is stubborn, and pig-headed. He won't give up easily."

"I hope you are right." Gwen looks at Merlin and mouths the words *'do something'*.

Merlin nods and leaves the room.

Bethany, and Gwen wait patiently for something to happen. They can tell Luthor is dreaming, or is he in pain? His eyes move back and forth quickly under his eyelids. Suddenly, Merlin comes bursting through the door.

"It's about time." Bethany blurts out. "It has been hours since you left."

"My lady, magic is not always instantaneous." He moves to Luthor's bedside.

Gwen moves out of the way and to the other side of the bed. Crawling in beside him, she sits close and waits to see what Merlin will do. He pulls a vile from his belt and uncorks it with a pop. The liquid, black and thick, smells like charcoal.

"What is it?"

"A mixture of charcoal, sulfur, sunflower, and oil." He pours it slowly into Luthor's mouth.

"What is it supposed to do?"

"It should induce vomiting, young one. If there is any poison left in his system, this may help flush some of it out. We will also need to drain his blood. It's a new operation I have seen to help clear any poison from the bloodstream." He stands back from Luthor, waiting for the potion to act.

Something that should be instant, is taking too long. "Why is it not working?"

"I am not sure. It could be possible it only works when he is awake, and all his organs are functioning normally." Merlin becomes unsure of his actions.

"Well, let's do the blood thing."

"Yes, my lady. I will need a few things." Merlin begins to leave the room again.

Before he makes it out the door, Luthor's body begins to shake in a fit of rage. Foam rises from his lips, and he starts to gag, causing Merlin to rush to the bedside and instruct the girls on what to do next. "We need to get him on his side."

We turn Luthor, so he is on his right side, over the edge of the bed. The foam begins to turn to a more solidified liquid, and chucks fly from his mouth. Merlin jumps back, barely missing his cloak. Gwen does her best to hold him still through it all. As his body heaves and arches, it becomes difficult to keep her grasp. "How long will this last?"

"Could be minutes. It varies with each person." Merlin answers over the noise of the vomit hitting the floor.

Bethany watches as Luthor's eyes never open through the whole ordeal. How is he still not conscious? She really can't understand it. Trying to keep calm, she can't stop the tears from flowing.

At that moment Guinevak walks into the room. The horrified look on her face is enough to cause anyone to leave, but she doesn't. She continues to Bethany's side, and grabs onto her, holding her as tight as she can. "I am here."

Meanwhile, the knights gather around the Round Table. "Men." Lancelot calls for their attention, "we need to decide what to do if the king doesn't make it through this."

"This is not the time; we should be by his side, not acting like he is already dead." Gawain interrupts with frustration.

"No one is acting like the king is dead, but we must be prepared for the worst. He has no heir, and he has not married Guinevere. Which means if he perishes, there is no one to take the throne."

"What do you propose we do? There is no one else with a claim, at least none we know of."

"As you mention, Tristan, I propose when he wakes up enough to be coherent, we convince him and Lady Guinevere to marry immediately. If anything happens to him, she will become the rightful ruler and no decision will need to be made."

"Have you discussed this with her ladyship, and the pope?"

"I plan to once we come to an agreement, Gawain. So?"

"All in favor?"

"Aye."

Luthor has finally stopped heaving, and there is nothing else coming out of his mouth. Once we clean him off and change his clothes, we check his bandages and change them to cleaner ones. Servants are on their way to clean up the mess, and the ladies open the windows to get some fresh air and get rid of the smell.

Everyone leaves Luthor to rest, and by the end of it all, we notice his fever has broken finally. Merlin decides he will wait longer to see if it lets up completely before he draws the blood.

Lancelot meets Bethany and Gwen in the hallway. Stopping, he begs for an audience in the throne room. Not being asked before, Gwen is unsure of how to respond. Being reluctant, she follows him, with Bethany and Guinevak close behind.

It's not far from Luthor's chambers, and when we arrive, the knights are already there, lined the center of the room, with servants, noblemen, and women standing behind them.

"What is this?" Gwen is confused.

"Please." Lancelot motions for her to take one of the smaller seats on the platform.

"This is the seat of the queen, I can't sit here."

"Please." He begs again.

Gwen concedes and makes her way to the chair. Refusing to sit, she stands in front of it and awkwardly waves for Bethany and Guinevak to stand by her side.

Tristan moves forward as Lancelot takes his place in the line. "My lady, we have discussed what will be the outcome if our king doesn't survive."

Bethany raises a hand to stop him. "He will come out of this. There is no worry of this."

"We understand, my lady, but if something does happen to him, the people have decided." He looks around to the others in the room.

"Decided what?"

"No matter if you marry King Arthur or not, you will become queen upon his passing."

Shocked, she doesn't know what to say.

"What say you my lady?" A priest, quiet in the corner, speaks up. "You have the Pope's blessing."

"I." She looks at Guinevak and Bethany.

Once Gwen agrees, cheers ring out from everywhere in the room. Even though everyone else is happy, she knows this decision will mean the end of her being a Guardian for good. So, as she stands, staring at a sea of people, her heart begins to break knowing Luthor is not here with her to celebrate this decision. A sudden feeling of panic rises over her, and a gut feeling tells her she needs to be near him. "I am sorry, I need to go."

Bethany, Guinevak, and Angelic follow closely behind as she leaves the room and runs to Luthor. Swinging the door open, she catches his gaze before anyone else. His eyes are weak and barely open, but he is awake.

She rushes to the side of the bed, not even thinking about whether or not the mess has been cleaned up. Bethany crawls into the bed, and Angelic and Guinevak stand at the foot smiling.

"I've missed you."

"Ow!"

"Oh my god, I am so sorry. I am so happy you are finally awake."

"What happened?"

"You don't remember?"

"You were fighting Morgause and she stabbed you. You collapsed, and we have been trying to revive you for almost two days." Bethany does her best to stay calm.

He turns his head towards her and looks at her in wonder. She looks at him strangely, and she understands what he is thinking. She looks up at me with sad eyes, ready to cry.

"He has no idea who I am." She begins to whimper.

"You are one of the ladies in waiting, are you not?"

Bethany rushes from the bedside, and bursts from the room sobbing. All the while, Gwen brushes the top of my hand.

"I am feeling tired. I think I will try to sleep now." I begin to drift off again.

"Luthor."

"Who is Luthor?"

Gwen looks up at Merlin. "You are, you are Luthor."

"I am Arthur Pendragon, son of Uther."

"Yes, yes you are." She reassures me reluctantly. I begin to drift off again, and Gwen stops me. "Arthur!" I open my eyes as best I can. "I love you."

"I love you too, so will you marry me?"

"When you get better, we will have the biggest wedding Camelot has ever seen."

"Now." I stop coughing, "Right, now."

"But Arthur." I turn my head away from her, and she knows no argument will win. "Angelic, can you get the priest or Bishop or whatever?"

"Of course, Gwen."

"Thank you."

The bishop and priest both arrive, and thankfully, I am able to stay awake long enough for them to get here.

"Who will be your witnesses?" The priest looks around.

I lift a tired and heavy finger towards Bethany and Lancelot. They both step close to the bed, and I can barely make out their faces.

Looking around, everyone looks so somber and depressed. My thought is interrupted by the priest's words, "This is quite unorthodox your majesty."

"Please do it."

He turns to Gwen, "Are you ready my dear?"

"Yes."

The priest looks around at everyone in the room. By now, most of the knights have filed in, as well as a few nobles from the court. It's a packed room, and everyone in it knows the worst is coming.

"Blessed be." he starts.

"Blessed be." Everyone repeats.

"We are here today to join King Arthur and Guinevere together in holy matrimony. You have been asked here to share in their joy, and to declare their love for one another before you. Lord, art thou here this day in pledged troth of thy own free will and choice?"

"Yes, father."

"Lady Guinevere, art thou here this day in pledged troth of thy own free will and choice?"

"Yes, father."

"In as much as Arthur and Guinevere have pledged their troth to be married this day, we call upon Heaven to bless this union. Therefore, if anyone can show cause, why they may not be joined together, by God's Law, or the Laws of the Realm, let them now speak, or else hereafter be silent for all time." He pauses a moment to see if anyone will respond before going on. "There being no objection to this marriage, let's continue. Swear you now, there is no reason known to you that this union should not proceed."

"I do so swear."

"Is there any reason known to you why this partnership should not be made?" He turns to Guinevere.

"There is none."

"Heavenly Father, creator of all things in both heaven and earth, we humbly ask thee to bless this union, may your servants seek goodness all the days of their lives, may they be strong in defense of what is right and good, may they be united as one even as thou art with God. May they be numbered amongst thy sheep. We humbly pray in the name of the Father, and the Son and the Holy Spirit. Amen." He makes the sign of the cross.

"Is that it?"

"No, my lord."

"Please go on." I am beginning to feel weaker, and I want him to finish quickly.

"Do you, Arthur, take unto thyself as wife the fair Guinevere, and pledge unto her before God and these witnesses to be her protector, defender and sure resort; to honor and sustain her, in sickness and in health, in fair and in foul, with all thy worldly powers; to cherish and forsaking all others, keep thee only unto her, so long as ye both shall live?

"I will."

"Do you, Guinevere, take unto thyself His Royal Highness King Arthur to be thy rightful husband and pledge unto him before God and these witnesses; to honor and cherish him, to cleave unto him, in sickness and in health, in fair and in foul, be his one true and lasting counselor and solace, and forsaking all other, keep thee only unto him, so long as ye both shall live?"

"I will." Guinevere's voice becomes shaky, and I can feel her hands trembling.

"We will now perform the handfasting ritual where three cords will be placed over their joined hands. Lady Bethany, will you begin?"

Bethany places a burgundy cord to symbolize romance, partnership and happiness over our hands.

"Now Lady Ragnall."

Lady Ragnall places an ivory cord, which stands for peace, sincerity and devotion.

"Sir Lancelot?"

Lancelot places a gold cord, which represents unity, prosperity and longevity.

"With these cords, I bind together." He reaches for all three and ties them together above our hands. "As this knot is tied, so are your lives now bound as one. Woven into this cord, imbued into its very fibers, are all the hopes of thy friends and family, and of thyselves, for a new life together. With the fashioning of this knot, you tie all the desires, dreams, love, and happiness wished here in this place to your lives for as long as love shall last. In the joining of hands and the fashioning of a knot, so are your lives now bound, one to another. By this cord, you are now and forevermore bound to your vow. As your hands are bound by this cord, so is your partnership held by the symbol of this knot. Two entwined in love, bound by commitment and fear, sadness and joy, by hardship and victory, anger and reconciliation, all of which brings strength to this union. Hold tight to one another through both good times and bad and watch as your strength grows."

The bishop continues, "thou hast pledged love of thy own free will and sworn upon the vow. May it be granted what is done before the gods be not undone by any man. As I proclaim you joined, kiss three times. Once for luck."

Guinevere leans in and kisses me.

"Twice for love."

And again.

"Thrice for long life."

The third time she kisses me, I can feel a few tears hit my face. At this point I have no energy to even open my eyes. I can hear the words the bishop is saying, but the heaviness of my eyelids is too much to open them.

"By the power vested in me by the Holy Roman Catholic Church, I now pronounce you King Arthur and Lady Guinevere, husband and wife."

I can hear everyone applauding, and I feel her squeeze my hand. She leans in to give me a kiss, and I feel sadness at the fact she is kissing me in the state I am in.

I suddenly feel a quill in my hand and someone lays a piece of parchment on my chest. "Arthur, you need to sign this." Gwen whispers in my ear.

"Help me."

She holds my hand and helps me write my name.

Guinevere

I hold Luthor's hand for as long as I possibly can. Everyone has left the room, except Guinevak and Angelic. I know by the cold clamminess of his hands, it's only moments. As much as I want to scream and cry, I know I can't.

"Can you find Bethany? She needs to be here."

Angelic turns to find her. Meanwhile, Guinevak, who remains quiet and vigilant, moves to Gwen's side. "It was a nice ceremony."

"I know." I rest my forehead on Luthor's hands.

Bethany comes through the door, and crawls back into the bed. She allows herself to stop crying and lays down next to her brother. As she wraps her arms around his chest to hold him, I can see the feeling of cold run through her.

As we sit around him, we watch as his chest moves less and less. When I finally turn to kiss him one last time, he lets out a faint exhale and I know he is gone. I look up at

Bethany and our fingers intertwine, allowing us to let it all out. We continue to hold hands, while Guinevak embraces me and Angelic holds on to Bethany.

Once things calm down, we leave Luthor lying there. The apothecary, the priest, and the undertaker do what they have to do to prepare his body.

Once he is ready, they move him to the main throne room for viewing. There, his body is placed on a stone altar, draped in gold fabric. He is dressed in the same armor he wore for the funeral pyre of the knights, and his shield and sword are resting on his chest. A black velvet cloth covers the bottom half of his body. The large embroidered dragon stands out for everyone who passes by.

He finally wears the crown he has purposely neglected the whole time he has been here. I stand over him grieving, oblivious to everything else around me. When a hand touches my shoulder, I jump from the sudden feeling. Lifting my head, I turn to find some of the most unlikely allies I have ever come across. Zeus, Hera, Aphrodite, Hephaestus, Apollo, Artemis, and Hestia stand at the foot of the altar.

The sadness in their eyes matches exactly how I am feeling at this moment. No one says a word, but I know why they are here.

When Bethany comes into the room and sees them, Hestia is the first to approach her.

"You were Luthor's sister?"

"I am Luthor's sister." Bethany corrects her.

"My apologies. I am Hestia."

"It's nice to meet you."

"Please accept our condolences."

"Thank you."

"Hello little one." Zeus speaks next. "I want you to know your brother meant a great deal to us, and I am sure he meant to you. Know we are here if you ever need anything."

"Thank you."

They turn back to me, and Zeus approaches while everyone else stays back. "The offer stands, no matter what."

"I don't think I'll need it now."

The gods say their final goodbyes, and one by one, they dissipate. Before Zeus can go, I stop him. I can't get out what I want to say, but Zeus knows. "Anytime you need me."

"It was nice of them."

"Yeah."

"Do you think they will come from France too?"

"Of course we will." A male's voice speaks behind her.

"Athos!"

"Gwen." He reaches for me, pulling me in close.

"My condolences." Porthos reaches for me next.

Aramis and D'Artagnan turn to Bethany and bow. "My lady, we can't be sorrier to lose such a great soldier."

"Thank you."

"How did you know?"

"We have been in watch of you ever since you left, Luthor." Athos looks over at Angelic and winks.

"Angelic, have you been in contact with them?"

"Something I will teach you."

"He was born a hero and died a king." D'Artagnan calls as the four men draw their swords and place them in hand over Luthor's body.

"One for all and all for one."

Then one by one they withdraw and sheath them again. They walk out of the throne room in formation like always. The sound of their boots hitting the tile floor echoes throughout. One by one, they turn as they reach the doorway. They raise their rapiers in unison, creating a beautiful starburst.

"All for one."

"And one for all."

"Do we know where his journals and his watch are?"

"Everything personal to him is on his bed, Bethany."

"I think it's time we open the watch and locket."

"I think you're right."

"Angelic, can you grab the pocket watch?"

"Of course, Bethany." Angelic leaves to make her way to his room.

"Their reaction won't be good, Bethany."

"I am not as worried about it . There is something else we haven't talked about."

"Me."

"You."

"I know."

"They asked you to be queen if Luthor died, and you agreed. So you won't be coming back with me."

"So, you are going home?" I turn to face Bethany, her eyes begin to fill with tears. "I can't do this alone."

"You won't be alone. You will have a group of knights who will die for you, and a wizard that can do anything."

"Except save someone's life."

"It will be your greatest trial yet." Angelic comes back.

"Plus, you will always have a way back to me, like the Gods and the Musketeers."

"What are you going to do?"

"Finish school, learn to fight, and who knows, maybe I will have my first adventure."

"Don't get ahead of yourself." Angelic gives her the mom look.

"Party pooper." Bethany places the watch and the locket on the floor facing Luthor.

I bend down, and simultaneously, we push the buttons. The images of Catherine and Jason materialize before us, and the instant they see Luthor lying there, joy turns to pain.

Catherine looks to Bethany for an answer, while Jason stares at Luthor's body. "Poison." Bethany looks sadly at her mother.

"How? Who?"

"We were surprised by Morgause. The blade she had was poisoned. She stabbed Luthor three times with it.

Merlin did what he could to save him, but it didn't help." Bethany holds back the tears.

"Where is she now?"

"Stripped of her powers and locked away in a jar where she will never be free."

"I." Catherine turns to me.

"We are married now, and he died the king."

"So this means."

"I am the queen of Camelot."

"Are you not going back home?"

I look at Bethany and Angelic, and Jason instantly knows the answer.

"So, what will you do?"

"I will be crowned after the mourning period."

"Oh, my dear, sweet Gwen."

"Keep the watch."

"It's Luthor's."

"It's yours now. He will want to know you have it."

"Kiss him for me."

"I will."

"We love you." Catherine looks to Jason, then to Bethany and I.

"We love you too."

As Catherine's spirit cries silently, they fade away.

Luthor's body is moved from the throne room to the church. The bishop comes again, and this time he will be performing the King's burial rights. I sit in my black velvet dress; Bethany in something similar but trimmed in gold. Angelic stays in what she normally wears, and the knights now brand a black cape with the symbol of the gold dragon. Everyone who is attending the service is wearing some form of black, even the Musketeers and the Gods came back as promised.

I look at each of them and know in the short time Luthor was the traveler he has touched many lives and done great things *'no matter how stubborn or whiny he was about it.'* I laugh to myself.

My thoughts are interrupted when the bishop begins to speak. "The grace and peace of God our Father, who raised Jesus from the dead, be always with you." He continues in prayer while sprinkling Luthor's body with Holy Water. Like his mother, Luthor is now covered in a sheer white cloth.

"Brethren, let's acknowledge our sins, and so prepare ourselves to celebrate the sacred mysteries. I confess to thee almighty God and to you, my brethren, I have greatly sinned, in my thoughts and in my words; in what I have done and in what I have failed to do." Striking his chest he continues on; "mea culpa, mea culpa, mea maxima culpa Ideo precor beatam Mariam semper Virginem, omnes Angelos et Sanctos, et vos fratres, orare pro me ad Dominum Deum nostrum."

"Misereátur nostri omnípotens Deus et, dimíssis peccátis nostris, et perdúcat nos ad vitam aeternam." The others respond.

Bethany and I look around, confused.

"Amen. Stipendia enim peccati mors gratia autem Dei vita aeterna in Christo Iesu Domino nostro."

"Amen." Everyone calls out.

"Sicut pastor gregem suum pascet, in brachio suo congregabit agnos, et in sinu suo levabit fetas mecum quae."

"Amen."

The bishop catches my eye, and I give him a pleading look. Realizing I don't understand him, he switches to English. "I believe in one God, the Father almighty, maker of heaven and earth, of all things visible and invisible. I believe in one Lord Jesus Christ, the Only Begotten Son of God, born of the Father before all ages. God from God,

Light from Light, true God from true God, begotten, not made, consubstantial with the Father; through him all things are made. For us men and for our salvation he came down from heaven, and by the Holy Spirit's incarnate of the Virgin Mary, at the words follow up to and including and become man, all bow.

For our sake he was crucified under Pontius Pilate, he suffered death and is buried, and rose again on the third day in accordance with the Scriptures. He ascended into heaven and is seated at the right hand of the Father. He will come again in glory to judge the living and the dead and his kingdom will have no end."

The bishop then begins to pour wine into the chalice, speaking quietly; "By the mystery of this water and wine may we come to share in the divinity of Christ who humbled himself to share in our humanity." He raises the chalice above his head and continues, "Blessed are you, Lord God of all creation, for through your goodness we have received the wine we offer you;
fruit of the vine and work of human hands, it will become our spiritual drink." Then places the chalice back on the corporal and begins to chant to himself.

"Blessed be." Everyone calls out.

"Pater noster, qui es in caelis, sanctificetur nomen tuum. Adveniat regnum tuum. Fiat voluntas tua, sicut in caelo et in terra. Panem nostrum quotidianum da nobis hodie, et dimitte nobis debita nostra sicut et nos dimittimus debitoribus nostris. Et ne nos inducas in tentationem, sed libera nos a malo. Amen."

"Amen."

Communion follows, and since I have never done this before, I didn't know I was supposed to go first. The bishop gives communion to Bethany, Angelic, Guinevak, the Knights, and I. The Knights remain kneeling, facing Luthor while the bishop finishes.

"It's with great sorrow we lay thy brother to rest. Be with him oh Lord and keep his spirit free of sin and tyranny. Keep him safe in heaven and allow him your grace to become an angel among us."

"Amen."

Once the final amen is spoken, you can hear the rustling of clothing and big skirts in the pews. Everyone begins to leave the church, and no one but Angelic, Bethany, the knights, and I are left.

"Now what?"

"Now we take him and place him in the Mausoleum among his ancestors."

"And then?"

"And then we prepare for a coronation." He looks at me.

During the mourning period, I decide it is a good time to bring out the books and start my own entries. I kept about ten pages empty for the beginning, then start with where I am now.

Luthor is gone, the journals will pass on to Bethany, but not before I say my last words. I went through the typical periods of mourning for Luthor's death. Now I am considered the queen by marriage, I have to follow the proper protocol. Deep mourning period is the most intense. Thankfully I still had Bethany with me to have someone to go through it with. I had a few dresses made to last the two-week period. All black dress and no jewelry containing colored stones is what I am allowed to wear.

The next two weeks were half mourning, and I could switch to adding some white into the wardrobe. Each time I try to make things better for my emotions, someone will come to me with a problem, a solution, words of advice, or condolences. Honestly, all I want is to be left alone.

Finally, in week five, I transitioned into the period of second mourning. I am back to wearing mild colors mixed with black and white. This is the week I must get through before everything else changes for good. I will be crowned queen, Bethany and Angelic will go home, and I will be left in Camelot...alone.

There I stand, in the back of the throne room waiting to go in. I can hear the commotion through the double doors, and I know what I am about to do will be a huge step for me.

As the doors open, I make my way down the center aisle. Everyone rises to meet me as I pass. Bow after bow, you can hear the bustle of the skirts and petticoats rubbing against each other. A throne sits in front like it always does. I can see Bethany and Angelic dressed in royal gowns and covered in jewels. This is it, and there is no turning back. As I continue, I am greeted with, "Long live the Queen."

As I get to the front, I look over at the knights filling the first two pews. Their armor glistens in the sunlight, and I have never seen them so well groomed. Lancelot smiles, while Gawain and Tristan hold out a hand on each side of me, helping me up the stairs. Bethany and Angelic assist in moving the long train following my gown.

As I stand there with my back to everyone, the room becomes hushed in anticipation as the archbishop comes forward. I turn to face the audience with him beside me. "I am here before you on this day to become your queen. On this day, I will make my solemn vow to honor and carry out the traditions of Camelot."

The archbishop then takes over. "Anyone who feels the right is not valid may speak now."

There is nothing but silence from everyone as my nerves shake inside of me. I turn to the bishop and he begins the ceremony.

"My lords." the bishop turns to the nobles, "do you on this day acknowledge the undoubted Queen for all her rights and glory?"

"Aye."

Now comes the part I know will seal everything. He motions for me to kneel before him. "Will you solemnly promise and swear to govern thy peoples of Camelot and of your possessions and other territories to any of them belonging or pertaining, according to their respective laws and customs?"

"I solemnly promise so to do."

"Will you to your power cause law and justice, in mercy, to be executed in all your judgements?"

"I solemnly promise so to do."

"Will you to the utmost of your power maintain the Laws of God and the true profession of the Gospel? Will you to the utmost of your power maintain in Camelot, the protestant reformed religion established by law? Will you maintain and preserve inviolably, the settlement of the Church, and the doctrine, worship, discipline, and government thereof, as by law established? Will you preserve unto the bishops and clergy, and to the churches there committed to their charge, all such rights and privileges, as by law do or shall appertain to them or any of them?"

"I solemnly promise so to do."

I am then anointed with oil on my breasts and head as Bethany presents the crown to the bishop. As a prayer is said softly, blessing the crown, he then motions for me to stand and face the audience. He moves behind me, lifting the crown high above my head. Lowering it slowly, he finishes the prayer.

With the crown on, he takes my hand and guides me to the throne. I turn again to the audience and sit slowly on the red cushion. I stare out at them all as he places a scepter in one hand and a dagger in the other. Pausing for a moment, he turns to the crown and proclaims, "Long live the Queen!"

The coronation part is finally over, and as the crowd chants, "Long live the Queen" I rise to meet them, but never moving from my spot. Thinking my nerves had subsided, I become even more nervous knowing soon Bethany and Angelic would be gone.

One by one, the knights come before me and kneel, all repeating the same phrase, one after the other.

"My queen, it is with you I pledge my loyalty and honor. You have my sword and my life."

After each one, I place out my hand, they kiss it, and the next one comes over. Once they are all finished, the noble men and their wives take their turn. Each male drops to one knee, while the ladies curtsy with their head lowered.

The only thing they say before moving on is, "long live the queen."

It seems to take forever as person after person stands, kneels, bows, curtsies, and speaks their words. Now that it is all done, I leave first with Bethany, Guinevak, and Angelic behind me carrying the train. Behind them are the knights, and behind them are the knights wives. Lastly, the noble men and women.

I retreat to my room to change into something simpler while the septar, dagger, and large crown are placed back where they belong. Before I enter the great call, a smaller, more subdued crown is placed on my head.

The double doors open and I stand waiting as everyone rises to their feet. Bethany, Guinevak, and Angelic are behind me again, but this time, no train. As I walk the long path to the front of the room, they bow and curtsy as I pass. Once to the head table, I stand at my seat facing everyone. Before I can sit to eat, everyone raises their glass to a toast.

"Long line the queen!"

It's now time for Bethany and Angelic to go back and I couldn't be more depressed about it. The last few days since the coronation have been so calm and peaceful with them here. I have no idea what I am going to do when they are gone for good. Oh sure, Angelic said I can pop back and forth, but since time runs differently, I am going to miss so much. Did I make the right decision?

"Of course, you did." Bethany hugs me.

"Reading my mind?"

"I don't have to. Trust me, it's all over your face."

"I am sure it is."

Bethany backs away and Angelic comes in for a hug. "Take care of yourself. If you need anything." She trails off. I feel something in my hands and she slowly backs away.

I look down to find a small broach glistening in the sunlight. A picture of a cursive 'T' in the center, surrounded by purple stones. I look up at Angelic and she smiles. Raising her right hand, she pinches 2 fingers together. "Anytime you need me."

I smile back and place the broach on my dress. When I look up again, both of them are standing there, happy and sad expressions on their faces. Behind me, I can hear the knights shuffle their way forward. One by one they kneel in front of Bethany and Angelic, taking each of their hands and kissing it, with a plethora of 'your grace' and 'my lady'. Lancelot, being the last one, hands Bethany something but I can't see what it's. She acknowledges him and he moves back in line behind me. She tucks it in her pocket and I move closer to them, the bottom of my skirt brushing the dusty ground.

"I love you with all my heart." I take Bethany in my arms again.

"I love you too."

I look over at Angelic and beg her to take care of her. "Without hesitation, your grace."

Angelic looks over at Bethany, she takes Angelic's hand, they close their eyes, and without a moment more, they are gone.

I turn to the men, and with my first royal duty as queen, I call a meeting at the Round Table.

Bethany

I have been writing in these journals since Luthor died. It's only right I finish his story since he can't. Gwen made me promise before I left Camelot I would guard them with every fiber of my being. It was hard saying goodbye to both of them, but I knew I needed to come back.

So much has changed in the past few weeks, and I think I have come out of it a completely different person. It will be rough for a while, not having my brother and Gwen here with me. I guess the good and the bad news is Angelic will be moving into this apartment. Everything Guardian related will come here, and everything else is in her apartment now will be donated to a needy family. Since we have all the furniture and everything we need, might as well let someone who needs it have it.

As for Gwen and Luthor's things, that's a different story. Gwen will be able to come back for a day to get her stuff, but she will not be bringing any clothes, just some personal items. Everything else is going to be donated along with Luthor's. I am sure there are some things I will keep, and so will she, mementos and all kinds of things. His watch was buried with him, but before, even though my father asked Gwen to keep it. I now have possession of the sword, and I found the ring in a box under his bed. It now sits on a chain around my neck with the locket..

I think I am about all cried out for now. I am not saying it won't happen anymore, but for now, I am good. Angelic took care of everything at school. They were able to arrange it so I was only gone for about a week's time, and I can make up any work I missed. They know about Luthor, and they think Gwen moved away after his death. Once their diplomas come in the mail, I will keep Luthor's and I will figure out a way to get Gwen hers.

I miss it already, to be honest. Part of me wanted to stay with Gwen in Camelot, but I know deep down there is work to be done. Angelic says I will be training more vigorously from here on out, and I may have convinced her to have me home schooled for the rest of my high school career. It's a work in progress though. I found out the Guiney I know, my best friend, would not be there anyway. As for the winter ball, well I guess I will have to go back to Camelot. Leave it to Gawain to pull a stunt like this.

I know once I close the book it means it's the end of another chapter. Part of me doesn't want it, but part of me knows another chapter means new adventures. To that I say, bring it.

Well, I smell dinner. Good night Luthor. Good night Gwen.

Bethany- Luthor's baby sister.

Mr. Fisher- Biology teacher and manifestation of the Fisher King.

Fisher King- A king encountered during the Quest for the Holy Grail.

Gabriel- A school kid with a crush on Bethany and manifestation of Gawain.

Gawain- Gawain resides as the nephew of Arthur; his parents, Lot of Orkney and Morgause. Upon the death of his father, he became the head of the Orkney clan, which includes many of his brothers and their wives.

Gwen-Luthor's best friend with a manifestation of her own.

Guinevere- she is beautiful and desirable. It's unknown whether she was forced into or conceived and engineered the extra-marital relationship with Lancelot and later condemned, causing her to repent and join a convent.

Guiney-Bethany's best friend and a manifestation of Guinevak.

Guinevak-Sister to Guinevere. She is fierce in her own right. Having battled demons of her own, while doing her best to live a good life.

Luthor-The protagonist of the story with a manifestation of his own.

King Arthur- King Arthur is best known for his leadership abilities, his loving rule, and his ruthless judgment of the affair between Lancelot and Guinevere. An important thing to remember about Arthur's life is usually forgotten: his skills as a general and knight.

Ms. Reigina- A teacher and the manifestation of Lady Ragnall.

Lady Ragnall- Lady Ragnall claimed Arthur's loyal knight Sir Gawain as her husband, after saving his life guised as a hag. Gawain reluctantly agreed, and on their wedding night, Ragnall reveals herself to be a beautiful maiden suffering a fearful enchantment. She must be a hideous hag half the day, a beautiful maiden the other.

Lady of the Lake- This mysterious female gave Arthur his sword, Excalibur. She stole Lancelot when he was a child and cured him when he went mad.

Mr. Lancaster- The science teacher and the manifestation of Lancelot.

Lancelot- Tell us of the love and I will tell you of Lancelot and Queen Guinevere. Lancelot rescued Guinevere from the stake on two different occasions. It was the second time he rescued her Lancelot killed Sir Gareth, mistakenly, leading to the disbandment of the Round Table. Upon the Queen's repent, Lancelot lived the rest of his life as a hermit in penitence.

Melvin- A know-it-all student with the manifestation of Merlin.

Merlin- Arthur's adviser, prophet and magician.

Ms. Easegrom-The school nurse with the manifestation of Morgause.

Morgause- The half-sister to Arthur. She married Lot, and mothered Gawain, a Knight of the round table.

Mrs. Granada - A teacher and manifestation of Morgana.

Morgana- Sister to King Arthur and also known as Morgan le Fay. She was skilled in magic of all sorts, and despised Arthur for slaying the man she loved in battle. To gain her own ends, and revenge herself upon the King, she kept a smiling face, and let none guess the passion in her heart.

Mr. Testerman- The principle and manifestation of Tristan

Tristan- Tristan was a contemporary to King Arthur and a Knight of the Round Table; nephew and champion of King Mark of Cornwall, and the son of Meliodas, King of Lyoness. Upon his mother's death when he was born, he later took service with his uncle, Mark.

Anna, Carmen, James, Michael, Joshua, Lyndsay, Donna, Cristine, and Kristen-Students in Mr. Fisher's class with no ties to alternate spirits.

Christina, Steven, Diana, and Michael-Angelic's brothers and sisters.

About the Author

C. J. Rose resides in Central Illinois; originally from just south of Chicago. The passion for writing took root in high school where she began writing song lyrics and poetry. C.J. found her inspiration from other fantasy and YA novels such as Percy Jackson, Harry Potter, Chronicles of Narnia, and more. On top of literature, Rose has a keen love for all things nerdy and sci-fi. On a quiet night, you can find her curled up with an episode of Doctor Who, Arrow, Firefly, and more.

Made in the USA
Monee, IL
26 May 2022

97086724R10194